Colton

THE FOUND BY YOU SERIES: BOOK SEVEN

VICTORIA H SMITH

COLTON: BLAKE: The Found by You Series: Book Seven

Copyright © 2019 by Victoria H. Smith

All rights reserved. No part of this book may be reproduced or transmitted in any form, including electronic or mechanical, without written permission from the publisher, except in the case of brief quotations embodied in critical articles or reviews.

This book is a work of fiction and any resemblance to any person, living or dead, any place, events or occurrences, is purely coincidental and not intended by the author.

Edits by **Straight on 'til Morningside and Judy's Proofreading**

One

CAMI

I PUSHED my way through the grinding bodies, shaking my head at the familiar situation I just lodged myself into.

He's going to get the cops called on his ass again.

A beefy arm came out like a grapple hook from my right, and my heels flew out from underneath me. A startled screech left my throat, and I was lodged into the side of a body about seven feet tall to my five foot five. I didn't know this guy, but he sure acted like he knew me, breathing a cloud of thick yeasty breath in my face. My boss sure hung out with the best.

Embedding my fingers into my leather bag, I prepared to use it to slap the shit out of the guy who was all hands and no manners, but another guy matching his height with a slimmer physique separated us. Basketball players littered the site tonight. After all, I did *work for* a basketball player, but at least this was one I could handle.

Jesse managed to get that asshat off me, beer in hand while he did so. He shoved him once I was free. "Watch it, douche."

The guy simply shrugged the encounter off, moving into a groove put on from the speakers that lined the house, which was located in the Hills. Embedded deep in the landscapes of palm trees and scenery, the LA home had a semblance of seclusion from the rest of the world, but it wasn't like neighbors weren't around to hear all this bullshit happening tonight.

He's really going to get the cops called on him.

I brushed my latest tussle off. I had about three since I walked in already. Jesse fought to keep himself from snorting while I got my blouse together, but hid it behind his beer bottle.

"You all right?" he asked behind brown eyes.

I rolled mine, shrugging my bag up my arm. "I could have handled that."

"Oh, no doubt. I was saving him from you and your handbag, slugger."

And he knew I was capable of doing some damage too. I had before. Not like I had been given a choice. When were parties *not* happening here?

I gazed around, my arms crossed. "Where is he?"

By *he*, Jesse knew exactly to whom I referred. He raised his beer bottle to the room of thrashing bodies. "Enjoying the rewards of his hard-earned work. It's not every day a guy's got one of the hottest teams in the league after him. He's taking it easy tonight."

The audacity of it all had me throwing my head back. "Kind of early to be celebrating when the papers aren't even signed."

True, my boss got an offer. His dream team really and many more on the table as he was the most sought-after free agent in the game right now. Colton Chandler was the player everyone wanted to get their hands on and would fight tooth and nail to get, his rising stats and skills well known since his debut only a few years ago. Because of that, he got the pick of the litter as far as teams went once his latest contract was up. But none of that would matter if he couldn't even take a moment to make things legal. His brother's team was waiting on an answer, the one he ultimately chose.

I wished I could say this had been the only "celebratory" party, but Colton had *just* gotten off a plane after the first. Once he got the big news about Miami coming for him, his family threw a huge shindig in his hometown back in Texas for him, something he'd barely been spotted at once he got there. I knew because I'd been on the front lines as his assistant, and my boss had basically gone AWOL, *myself* having to dodge questions left and right from his own frickin' family about where the star was. I didn't really get to see him until we left.

He threw *this* party barely after the plane's wheels hit the tarmac upon coming home to California.

Jesse drew an arm around my neck, the only one who could pull that off and knew the gesture wouldn't be met with a fresh hand to the face. Jesse Michaels was actually one of Colton's friends I could stand, but he'd be wise not to test me now, his friend literally all over the place as of late. Colton's agent, Joe, had been trying to get ahold of him since we got back as Miami really was waiting. They needed to hammer out when he'd sign the paperwork, but that couldn't be done if the "star player" couldn't be found.

Jesse flashed deep brown eyes at me from under lengthy brown strands. "*Relax*, Cami. Take a night off and let the paperwork wait. Everyone's here tonight to celebrate with Colt, and you should too. You're a part of it."

The reason I had a job was because I *didn't* participate in things like this and kept my boss in line. Someone had to be responsible for Colton Chandler when he wouldn't be for himself.

I slid from under his arm, my smile tight. "Colton, Jesse. Just Colton. I know you know where he is."

The smile left his lips. Raising the beer bottle toward his

mouth, he flicked it in a random direction before taking a sip. "Off getting some pussy somewhere, I think."

I fought myself to keep from groaning. It wouldn't be the first time I'd have to break that up to get him to handle his responsibilities. I supposed tonight would be yet another night.

The bottle left Jesse's lips when he lowered it. "I'd check his room." The words had barely left Jesse's mouth before his long reach found a redhead, his lips to her neck. "Hey, baby. Join me for a drink somewhere."

The two left me in the crowded living room, and I could only shake my head. Colton with a girl meant Jesse had to have two to his one. He grabbed another on his way out to the deck overlooking the pool. I'd never get over guys having to one-up the other.

My heels trekked up the spiral staircase. Colton's *guests* were making full use of the wet bar on level two. He let these people suck him dry, but then again, that's how people like him operated. The rich were an entirely different breed, a fact I knew too well.

A girl passed out in the stairwell caused me to snarl my lip. I passed over her and headed down to Colton's room. He'd be handling that one pronto. He did *not* need a potential sexual assault case happening in his home.

My fist drummed against the wide door, hoping he at least had his clothes on when he answered the door this time. Last time had been... questionable.

The door opened, and my back stiffened at the half-naked girl on the other side. Colton's type for sure, leggy and beautiful as she buttoned up her shorts. But that's not why my back went up. It was the fear in her eyes, and the stream of tears she had in a thick trail of mascara running down a set of flushed cheeks. Her front bare, she had a shirt pressed up against her naked breasts.

She sniffed. "I told him not to take so much."

That's all she said. That's all she got out before rushing away from me and fleeing down the hallway.

A sprinkle of scattered clothing led to Colton's bed, and the sight on top made my bag fall from my shoulder and my stomach toss as my pulse ticked rapidly in my neck.

Colton wore nothing but boxer briefs on his extensive frame, similar to the girl and her near nakedness in that aspect, but there was a difference, a vast one that made the world spin where I stood.

A single body did nothing but thrash in his bed, convulse. His mouth was open, the sheets bunching under his shaking frame and a table with white scattered powder told me why, a couple rolled dollar bills beside them.

Oh my God.

I rushed to his side, my own hands shaking as I picked up his cellphone, lying haphazardly next to the splatter of drugs. His eyes had turned white, what I knew to be bright blue irises lost as they'd rolled back in his head.

"911, what's your emergency?"

My hand hovered over him, his body that wouldn't stop moving, wouldn't stop shaking. I stared at the powder, a thin trail remaining from what I assumed were snorted lines. There were so many, so many.

"911, please state your emergency."

His skin paled, his body white, and next to him was an empty pill bottle, the tiny capsules from inside strewn about underneath his arms.

What are you doing? You don't...

"911, please—"

"It's my boss," I said, pressing the phone to my ear. "It's my boss. He took something. I don't know what. He's shaking. Please help me."

"Where are you located, ma'am?"

"In the Hills," I said, rattling off the address next. This didn't make sense. This was a dream.

"I'm sending an ambulance, ma'am," said the dispatcher. "Can you tell me your name?"

"Camille," I flustered. "Cami. This man is my boss. His name is Colton Chandler, and he's convulsing. His skin, it's…"

A body that used to be tan thrashed so hard beside me. His arm shot out in a broken-like position, and then a thick foam trickled from his open mouth.

My breath left me.

"He's vomiting! Oh, God. He's vomiting. Help me, please!"

"Okay, Cami. I'm going to need you to turn his head. Don't hold his arms or keep him from moving. Just turn it so he doesn't choke."

Moving on the bed, my hand slid under thick blond curls. Upon turning his head, the pink liquid in his mouth spilled, staining the white pillow beneath him. So much seeped out but he didn't gag on it. I kept his head turned until he stopped.

"Is he still vomiting, Cami?"

I shook my head like she could see. "No, but he's still moving. I think he's having a seizure."

But he was alive. He was alive.

"Just don't touch him, Cami. Is he in a position to injure himself?"

I eyed him. "No."

"Good. Can you tell me Colton's height and weight? His age?"

"He's twenty-six. Just had a birthday and…" My brain reached for other information, things I should know backwards and forwards. I knew everything about this man. I was paid to know, but in that moment, it all fuzzed like a thick cloud in my mind.

Lines. So many lines were on that table.

I rattled off six foot five and his weight. I had no idea how close I was on the latter with the fog in my rattled brain. "He plays basketball professionally."

"Thank you, Cami. Can you tell me what you think he took?"

Pills around him lay scattered from an unlabeled bottle, the lines of drugs foreign to me as well. Could have been coke, could have been something else, but Colton didn't do drugs. He didn't... and then, the bottle of vodka took my attention, the glass shattered in a million pieces on the floor. He took all this.

He ingested it all.

"Cami, please tell me what you think he took. Describe it for me. I need you to be my eyes."

I turned as flashing lights sprinkled the room through the bedroom's wide window, cops unloading from the very cars that held them below. Moving, I saw no ambulance, only a police response.

A response to a party.

He really did get the cops called on him.

"Cami?"

The strain of the voice took my attention, the weakness in a familiar depth.

The tremors had left Colton's big body, the seizure abated. Eyes roaming, he couldn't focus on me, his lids opening and closing, but he said my name. I know he did.

I leaned in, touching his silky curls. I never touched him like this before, his hair so soft.

"Colton?" I asked, searching for his eyes. I found him when that ray of blue finally made its way toward me. He found me and when he did, his expression cringed into something tortuous I didn't understand, the agony in his eyes not far behind.

"Don't," he started, reaching for me before he closed his eyes. "Don't tell my family. Don't tell them. Don't tell them..."

He just kept saying that over and over, to not tell his family, to keep to myself about what was happening.

I gazed around, the booze and drugs filling my eyes before I faced him. His breath steady, no other words but those continued to leave his lips.

"Don't tell them," he gasped, his voice weak. "Don't tell them."

The drugs surrounded him, emergency services in my ears, but all I could hear was Colton, his desperate plea rising above all else and as I took in the reality of what he did and to the extreme lengths he did them, all I could think was one thing...

What exactly was he asking me not to tell?

Several Weeks Later

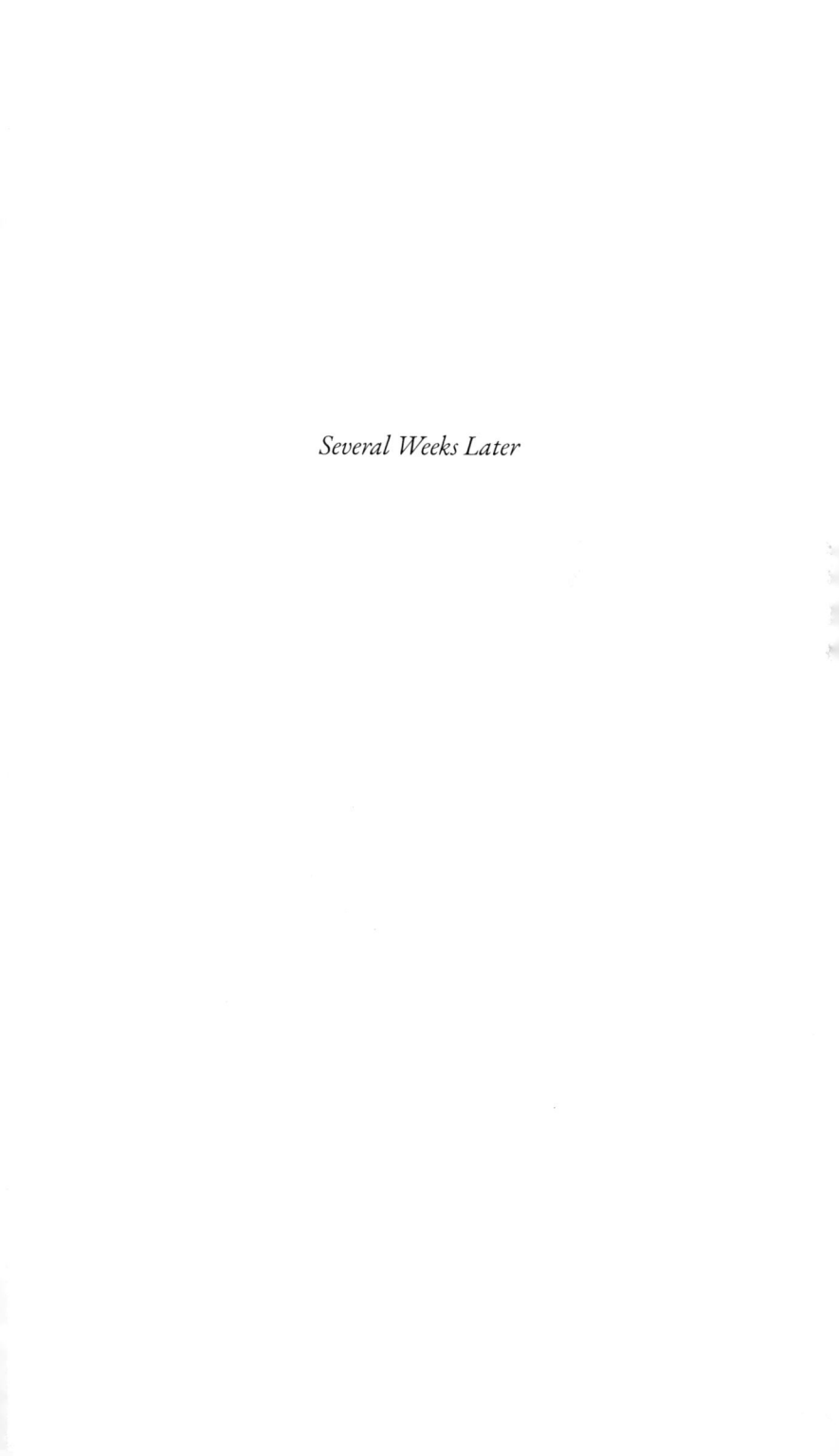

Two

COLTON

THIRTY DAYS. Thirty days of long nights, afternoons, mornings. For thirty days, I'd been removed from my life. I guess I should consider myself lucky, though. If the judge had it his way, I would've gotten ninety.

I braced myself as the jet's wheels hit tarmac, the sun casting its glow on the wide runway of LAX. I didn't know what awaited me after I left this seat, but I had an idea. I was given my personal items on the way out of Shining Hope, the place I'd been crashing at for some of the worst days of my life. How ironic a guy could be sent to rehab when he'd only taken hard drugs once in his life.

I slid my ball cap on, squeezing the bill before exiting the plane with my bag. The flight attendant handed me off to an escort, not unusual as someone went with me everywhere. Two bodyguards flanked behind me, and I fell into a place of familiarity. I really was home. If the men in black didn't tell me that, the photographers at baggage claim did.

I bypassed the flashing lights entirely, covering my eyes as a black Suburban pulled up in front of me. The windows were tinted, the inside unidentifiable, and a sudden wave of nausea warped me. Beads of sweat misted my brow, my hands clammy like just before an intense game.

Is she... in there?

The door opened from the inside, and I was relieved as much as I was anxious. Deep brown eyes and the curly dark lashes surrounding them I evaded for now, but that just meant more time would pass between us. It was time I needed to address sooner rather than later if only for my anxiety.

The assistant to my assistant, Tommy, hopped out of the ride, feeling the need to bow for some reason with his clipboard. He grinned. "Mr. Chandler, welcome back."

Mr. Chandler was my pop. Not me in all of my twentysomething years. I threw my bag over my back, nodding before hopping inside the SUV. I expected Tommy to join me right after and inquire about something as soon as he did, something about me. He might have, but he never got the chance.

Familiar hands, my stylist Margy, approached me immediately in the back of the car. Comb in hand, she whipped my hat off to take a comb to my head. Little did my stylist know, I went through some changes in rehab.

In more ways than one.

The stylist blanched at a shaved head. I guess you could call it an act of rebellion for having to serve time at a place I didn't belong.

I took the hat back, but she wouldn't let me return it to my head. Making do with what she had, she exchanged the comb for a thick bristle brush. She moved that brush over my head, and my other stylist Josie—also in the vehicle—attempted to rip my hoodie off, holding up a suit jacket to replace it. I eyed Tommy.

He simply smiled. "Joe's scheduled a press conference for you. You know, to make a statement."

I could think of a few choice words, but I kept them to

myself, knowing Joe's way. My agent, Joe Martina, didn't waste time when it came to me. He knew my aversion to the press so he forced me to deal with them like ripping off a Band-Aid. I loved the guy and had worked with him for a long time. He'd been a referral through my sister-in-law's firm. Vetted and all that, but that didn't mean he didn't bug the piss out of me sometimes with his brash techniques.

I moved back from all the hands on me. "I don't feel like dealing with the press today."

A flash of panic touched Tommy's face, and I knew I just hit him with defiance he wasn't equipped to handle. There was a reason he was assistant to my assistant. He lacked the iron stomach for this job. That came from someone else. Someone else who wasn't here for some reason. Tommy opened his mouth. "I understand, Mr. Chandler. But Joe said..." He paused, hesitant to argue. "Joe just wants you to get this out of the way so you don't have to deal with it. And Camille, she's tasked me with getting you there on time and ready. I've been informed the press conference won't take long and will have hardly any questions."

Cami. I raised my hand, giving up. "I'll go. Fine." She'd be there, no doubt. That's probably why she wasn't escorting me today, preparing for this thing.

I could get it all over with.

The color returned to Tommy's face now that I wasn't arguing. He nodded with a grin. "Thank you. And I like the new look. Very different but good."

I moved a hand over my buzz cut, a smile on my lips at this guy. "Thanks."

The team did what they could in the back seat of a moving vehicle. I was glad I thought to shave before leaving Shining Hope so I didn't look completely homeless. We pulled up to the Four Seasons, to the back I assumed because of the press. Another bodyguard was there to meet me, opening the door and letting me out. Tommy got ahead, looking kind of flushed without Camille by his side, and I didn't blame him. She kept things together. She was so good at that.

"*Colton?*"

I still remember the way she stared in my eyes that night. It haunted my dreams actually nightly. Her hand on my cheek, her small fingers in the hair I used to have...

"Mr. Chandler?"

I'd stopped, Tommy standing before me. That panic creeped up his cheeks in more flush. Putting a foot in front of me, I kept on, about to meet my maker in front of only God knew who. Outside of the airport, I hadn't had to deal with any press for so long. I watched for Cami during my strides, my hands damp for some reason, my mouth dry, but I didn't see her.

I grabbed Tommy once inside. "Where's—"

"Son."

My hand was grabbed—a distinguished black man, the owner. My agent, Joe, brought me in, trumping my blazer with his tailored suit.

I returned the handshake, surprised that his presence brought even the smallest relief. The last thirty days had been long, so long, and I was happy to find a trusting face.

"Glad to see you're no longer on the mend," he said.

Yeah, no longer.

He slapped my back, pulling away. "You look good."

I made sure of that before I left rehab. I'd been bad at that before I left, and I wouldn't do it again. Not again.

He squeezed my shoulder. "Let's go do this thing. Get it all out, and then, you can go home. We'll talk details later."

Details. The harsh reality of what I could have fucked up because of what I did hit me, but I swallowed it down as I nodded for Joe. He led the party off, but I noticed we were minus one. Cami. Where's Cami?

No one had answers for my internal questions, and I was led off to a door, bantering going on behind it. I could only assume the source was the press.

Joe turned to me. "Just read the prompters. They'll tell you everything you need. I won't allow any questions."

Due to the obvious situation. He left that part out though. I was grateful. He opened the door, saying he'd go in first before bringing me on. He spoke a few words, saying I was here to make a statement only and wouldn't be answering any questions. Turning, he gestured toward me, but I eyed Tommy.

"Where's Cami?" I asked him. Joe waved again, but I needed an answer.

Tommy looked up, shaking his head. "Oh, um, she's at her apartment. There was an issue, so I volunteered in her place."

Issue? What issue? I wanted to know, but Joe Martina was figuratively going blue in the face. I went out, and shutters blinded me. Almost instantly, the press ignored Joe's words. They fired off questions I wasn't at all equipped to answer.

"What's the story, Colton?" came one. "Will the judge's sentence affect your contract negotiations?"

The ultimate question, and one I had no idea how to answer even if Joe allowed that today. I had been in talks to sign with a new team. I received many offers after paying my dues on the court for the past some odd years, but the ultimate plan had been to settle on one in particular. Miami had sought me out among the lot, and the pressure and understanding was there to commit to them. They pursued me before I went pro, but I wanted to earn that right before joining them. That had always been the plan. Especially since that was the team my brother played for.

My older brother Griffin had a legacy in Miami since he started several years ago. He worked hard, made his mark, and the world, as well as our family, wanted us to play together for those last few years he'd be burning up the court. He was choosing to retire early and had been preparing for it for quite some time. He had a young family with my sister-in-law and had stake in her business, as well as my family's furniture business. His passion stayed with basketball, but his heart had always remained solid in family. In Miami, he would ride it out to the end and was supposed to pass the baton, his legacy there, to me.

At least, he was supposed to before all the crap with me went down.

The questions rang, but Joe held up his hand, denying them. He leaned in. "All questions about Colton's contracts will be addressed in the near future. Colton's here just to make an official statement today. So please hold your questions."

He gave the floor to me, whispering, "Prompter," before he did, and I saw that prompter. I saw the show I was required to put on.

I adjusted the mic. I was taller than Joe.

"I want to start by thanking Judge Fulton," I started reading the green-lit words. "Because without him, his sentence, I might not have gotten the resources I needed to address what happened. I might not ever have addressed my... my issue."

The words tasted funny in my mouth, the bullshit, and I chose to ultimately amend that last word—addiction. I wouldn't say that word written for me to say about myself. I wouldn't say it because it wasn't true. I went on.

"My struggles with..." There went that word again. I skipped it. "My issues have been hard and my time at Shining Hope helped me reflect upon it in ways I never would have without being forced to call attention to it. In so many words, the judge saved my life and I thank him for that."

I felt like a puppet, spouting off crap that the press was shoveling and documenting up with their cameras and notepads. All that judge did was crack down on something he thought he understood. He thought he knew me, a young athlete who got himself in too deep with the drugs. That's what he got me for, drugs, and the noise complaint made on my house that night only made it easy for him. I got slapped with a huge fine, but no jail time... as long as I went to rehab.

My gram had cried at the news. She was the strongest woman I knew and never broke down. But that day she found out I was going to rehab, she did. She did the day she believed I had become an addict.

An addict.

Just like her daughter.

That word, that belief, hurt even still, which was why I wouldn't say it today, skipping over it. Dampening my lips, I went on with the fodder, thanking the law for doing their duty. I let the press believe I learned something. I convinced them that those thirty days had been meaningful and not me dodging every answer my counselors at Shining Hope had tried to get out of me. Because that's all I did while I was there. I served time as if jailed, and once gone, I went back to my real job. I went back to my life.

I read the script. I went along with it because those words allowed me to have the life I worked so hard for back. Words I could do. Convincing the media, and even my family, was something I could handle. She'd made sure that I could, Cami. She'd written these words for me to say today, her style and the delivery of them was the easy part.

My only worry lay with the woman who I knew provided the script.

Three

CAMI

THE CEILING COLLAPSING ONLY ADDED to the nightmare. In a steady river, it fell to my bedspread, exploding in a pool of liquid I had no desire of knowing the source behind.

An ache left my throat watching my silk sheets, drenched in murky water from the apartment above me. Pressing my hand to my brow, I whipped around, and the only thing I got from my super was a cringe from behind his clipboard. His chubby fingers marked something down on the paper that better be a note for reimbursement for yet more of my personal property damaged by his. The only room in my apartment that *wasn't* flooded from his pipes bursting was, ironically enough, the bathroom.

I dropped my arms. "When is this going to be fixed?"

Hal did a shoulder wiggle, moving his fingers over a thick beard. "It's hard to say," he said, which in Hal speak meant several short millennia. He still hadn't fixed my fridge and I'd lived here for a few years now.

I guess the joke was on me.

In a huff, I reached for the edge of my bedspread to take off and wash, but then thought better of it.

You lived a long life, Ms. Wang. My Vera had traveled with me since my time in New York City. I supposed most things I left behind anyway.

Pushing my curls behind my ear, I stalked the expanse of my apartment, Hal taking note of all areas affected by the flooding—which was everything, but he had to officially document everything as my landlord. He snapped a couple pictures with his cellphone before meeting me at the door, the setting California sun bleeding its light into my dampened apartment.

"Of course I won't be charging you during your time away," he said, pushing his pencil behind an ear. That's the only place he had a little bit of hair. It came in small patches out of his earlobes and the sides of his head. Like any at all was better than nothing. He sniffed, clearing his throat. "You can use the money for where you'll be staying."

I forced a smile. "How generous, Hal. I appreciate that." And a healthy lump sum for the property damage, but I kept that to myself.

He nodded, backing away. "I'll keep you updated. We should be able to get the place back in tiptop shape real soon for ya." His face screwed up a bit like he was unsure of the very statement he just made. His confidence also must have left him completely because he scurried away, the rubber soles of his shoes squishing on my carpet when he fled.

A little cry escaping, I turned on my sneaker to salvage what I could of the rest of my stuff. Check-in at my hotel wasn't until four so I still had an hour or so to fill my car. I managed to get a pretty good deal at an extended stay with a few faux crocodile tears for my reasons of quick need, but even still, I was paying a small fortune. I could imagine hiring a surrogate to carry my child for nine months would have been cheaper.

That's what you get for trying to be cheap, Cami.

Well, I was definitely paying for that decision now. I left a dark trail of footprints from my travels in the sopping wet living room to my bedroom, but my concerns for the carpet were very little at this point. Half the contents of my apartment would need to be replaced.

Sighing, I grabbed the most important things—my clothes. I filled the trunk of my Jetta with those alone, so by the time I went back to my closet I was forced to play the game of what I really needed. I chose memories over comfort, grabbing photos of my family and some jewelry I got from my mom this past Christmas. Hal made it very clear whatever I couldn't take would be at the mercy of his restoration team so anything that looked even remotely expensive was either coming with me or going to the storage locker I rented this morning. I didn't need the electronics so my TV and things all went there. All that was left to go through were all the little nooks and crannies of the apartment.

I opened one of my dresser drawers, finding my stash of knickknacks and papers. It was essentially a junk drawer, but something caught my eye, a picture.

I pulled it out, resting my hip against my bedpost. In a wide ballroom, the picture was one of the many events I was forced to work at as my job as a personal assistant, and the man I worked for stood beside me. Sandwiched between two basketball players, I stood, the wide birth of them both taking most of the photo's surface area. One was Jesse Michaels, power forward for LA, and the other was my boss, Colton Chandler. In a dark gray suit, he had his hand on my shoulder, his fingers ghost white on the skin exposed by my formal gown as he'd very much forced me to get in this photo with him and Jesse.

"Loosen up, Cami. It's just a picture," he'd whispered in my ear that day. But he'd always had a light voice, soft. I had never in my life heard Colton yell, and his whispers weren't that far off from his natural speaking voice.

Jesse took the selfie and I posed for it between the two, giving one of those smiles that said I had to be there but didn't mind that day.

My stomach flipped at what I had gotten out of today. Avoiding Colton's homecoming had definitely been strategic, and though I didn't plan the pipes bursting and destroying my stuff, it did give me an excuse for avoidance. I hadn't seen Colton in over thirty days.

And I didn't know what to say when I did.

Sliding the photo into the box, I further denied the inevitable. My assistant, Tommy, was me today, and a monkey could follow the directions I gave him. He couldn't mess up my instructions for Colton today even if he tried. "Pick him up," I told him. "Get him to his press conference." The final direction was to take him home, so it was foolproof, even for Tommy.

He'd do what I said, all right. Colton will be okay.

Convincing myself of the fact, I picked up the box. I underestimated its weight with all the stuff I'd thrown into it but managed to get it out of my bedroom.

That's as far as I got.

My feet wet, I tripped on a piece of raised, sopping carpet, but leveled out when a set of hands came underneath mine. I steadied, and over the box came these eyes, blue ones, *bright* ones that managed to catch every bit of that sun setting outside my open apartment door.

I jumped. "Colton!"

My hip hit my lamp on the couch and the bulb shattered when it hit the floor. I didn't want to add apartment fire to the mix, so I picked it up quickly and felt Colton's presence behind me the moment I stood.

"Are you okay?" he asked, drawling. Colton Chandler was from Texas, his origins much closer to this city than mine.

I pushed my hair back, turning around. Had I not seen those eyes at first, I might have questioned who this man in front of me was. Colton had a bit of scruff on his chin, five-o'clock shadow. Though, it wasn't unkempt. The kicker was his hair, though. He had it buzzed, faded low, as if in the military, and without his fluffy blond curls, the overall package made him seem older. He looked like he'd aged a couple solid years instead of the thirty days he spent away, but not in a bad way. He matured gracefully, reminiscent of a fine wine.

Blinking those thoughts away, I raised the lamp, laying it to rest against the wall. "What are you doing here?"

He set the box down. "You weren't at the press conference."

He'd come all the way here because of that?

I pushed back my hair. "I sent Tommy."

He nodded, taking a seat on the edge of my couch. He was so much bigger than it. "Yes, but you weren't there," he said, leveling that flare of blue at me. It was deep, intense.

Breaking away from it, I lifted my hands to the environment. "A little preoccupied, I guess."

By the way he surveyed the apartment with his gaze, one would think he just noticed. He frowned. "What happened?"

I blew out a breath, reaching to gather more things. "Pipes burst. I'm trying to salvage what I can." He watched me from behind, and I turned. "You can take it out of my salary if you want. Me not being there?"

He lifted his hand, shaking his buzzed head. "You know better, Cami. You're fine."

But was he? I watched him watching me, feeling pinned.

"How are you?" he asked, low like he was testing the air with the words, and maybe he was. We both knew the last circumstances in which we'd seen one another. The difference between him and me was he didn't have the memories burned into his brain from them. He didn't get to see his family, his large brood of normally happy family members gathered solemnly around his hospital bed. He didn't get the questions about what happened to him and was then forced to relay the details about how I found him.

He didn't get to see him dying.

"Good," I said because no one ever really wanted to know the real answer to that question.

His lips moved after that. Like he wanted to say something but couldn't. He dampened them. "Cami—"

I picked up the box at his feet, but then he stood, reminding me of something else.

How freaking tall he was, his legs were tree trunks as he stepped forward. Barely lowering, he took the box from my hands. "Where does this go?"

He followed me out to my car, the Jetta chirping via my key fob. I got the door for him and he shot the seat up, maneuvering to get the box in the back seat. With every shimmy, his back muscles moved, sliding along the cotton under his red t-shirt.

Swallowing, I stepped back a bit, his body covering me in shadow when he stood from the car. "Thanks."

"No problem," he said, pushing his hands into his athletic shorts. His steel calves flexed as he rocked back on the soles of his sneakers. "Where will you go?"

"Go?" I asked, blinking.

God, quit staring at him.

He smiled a little. Maybe he knew he caught me. He pointed behind to my apartment. "With your apartment being flooded."

Folding my arms, I fell against my car. "Hotel. I've got an extended stay."

His eyes narrowed. "For how long? No offense, but the place is kind of a mess."

"Oh, none at all," I said, raising my hands. "It's only where I live."

Titling his head, that smile went full. "You know what I meant."

I did, so I let it go. "No idea, and apparently neither does my super. He couldn't give me a time."

The pair of us stood there for a while, looking at anything but each other, and I had no idea what to make of that. I had no idea what to *do* with that. I had been working with Colton for a handful of years now. In fact, shortly after he hit the ground running in his career, and over that time, we fell into kind of a routine with each other. And though it was professional, it had never been awkward. It had never been this. I told him thank you for helping me with my box, then went inside to get the last of my stuff.

Gratefully, he didn't follow me.

On my way back to the front door, I stood, giving the apartment one last once-over. True, this place sucked, but it was home. It had been my home since I got to LA, and there was some sentimental value there. I flicked off the light, choosing to let nature take its course as I sought out other options. After this incident, it was probably time to seek out other options for living arrangements. I thought about that as I made my way out the door, but all thoughts left at the sight of an empty Jetta. The boxes in the front seat and back had all been removed.

I ran down the walk instantly, but a set of back muscles under a red t-shirt distracted me—mostly because the owner was the one who'd swiped my stuff.

His arms full, Colton was making a rotation from my Jetta to what I now discovered he drove here in. The luxury Beamer he purchased just earlier this year. He'd been excited about all the interest he had from other teams while he was coming to the end of his current contract. He was now filling that Beamer with *my* stuff, and I had no idea why.

I raced over. "What are you doing?" My eyes bugged out at all the boxes he'd gotten in while I'd been away.

Ignoring me, he hunkered down and grabbed the last box. "Getting your stuff. You're coming to live with me."

The laugh coughed out of my throat. "No, I'm not."

"Yes, you are," he said, securing the last box. "Car space is pretty tight, but I'll send Tommy to get the rest of your stuff."

He was sending Tommy. *My* Tommy to get my stuff. I shook my head. "Colton. I am *not* living with you."

Rising up, he actually took a moment to talk to me, laying his arm on the top of the vehicle. "Really? Because I think your stuff in my car means you are."

He bounced his eyebrows once at me, then left me, jaw slack, to move around his vehicle. After a moment, he noticed I wasn't closing his door with my stuff inside. Flicking the seat up, I wriggled one of the small boxes out of the back.

He sighed. "Cami..."

I stood with a huff. "I'm not living with you."

"No, you're not," he said. "You're *staying* with me until your apartment is fixed."

I lowered the box to the ground. Even small, it was kind of heavy. "That's a technicality, and like I told you, I've made other arrangements."

"Yeah, at a hotel whose cooking options probably don't go that far past a microwave and enough closet space to hold maybe one of your boxes."

How did he know?

"I've got the space," he continued. "I've got plenty of space, and you know that. Not to mention, I won't charge you. You won't have to give me a dime. Call it a friend helping a friend."

But we weren't friends. He was my boss, and that was the problem. I huffed. "I work for you. It would be completely inappropriate."

His grin went wiry. "Irene works for me, and she lives with me."

My face fell. "Your housekeeper doesn't count, and she has a family she goes home to on the weekends." And she was mature in age, and he was, well, not. I'd constantly be worried what I'd wear and how to act around him, or worried if he was walking around naked.

Yeah, I was not living with him. "I can't just do what I want if I'm worried about what you're doing."

"You won't be on the clock if you stay."

"That's not what I mean." I pressed my hands to my brow, exhausted with both him and the conversation.

His face went serious. "What exactly *do* you mean then?"

"What if I want to walk around... I don't know. In my underwear or something?"

He smiled again. "I won't stop you from doing that."

I bet he wouldn't. Exasperated, I grabbed my box, but Colton was out in the street before I could make it back to my Jetta. His hands covered mine, and I stopped, letting him hold me there.

Those lips lifted. "I was joking, Cami. But not about you doing what you want to do. We'll make house rules, stay in separate wings."

Because, yes, he did have those.

"We'll make this work," he said, reaching around my fingers and to my wrist when he squeezed. He took the box from me again. "I'll respect you," he went on. "I'll respect your privacy and whatever you need to feel comfortable. You won't have to change your routine. I have no intention to either."

Another reason this was a bad idea, *his routine*. I was already forced to submit to the extent of his lifestyle, aka women and lots of them. I was on the clock and saw him with his daily harem, and frankly, I didn't want to see all that up close and personal.

On the other hand, what he said sounded like such a sweet deal. No rent. Privacy...

I breathed, and he lowered, finding my eyes.

"You're thinking about it?"

And only thinking. I had some terms. "I do need that privacy."

"And you'll have that," he agreed. "I promise."

I chewed my lip. "And... I'd like there to be no parties. At least not every week." I amended the statement as the first sounded a bit restricting. He was giving me freedom, and in return, I was taking away his, and that didn't seem fair.

"I can do... one a month?"

I didn't plan on staying with him that long, but in the case I did, one a month was reasonable. But I had one more thing.

I swallowed. "I don't mind alcohol, but no more drugs. At least not on your end."

With that, I literally felt the air seep. It got tense, but I felt it needed to be said. He couldn't do drugs. He *wouldn't* do drugs. Not around me.

I couldn't go through that again.

"You have my promise," he said, but like his impulsive invitation, I didn't understand why.

Four

COLTON

I COULDN'T BREATHE, my lungs denying me air. The world faded into darkness, but it wasn't in the normal way as if I'd fallen into sleep. It was something else, and I gasped, forcing myself out of it like many nights. The room bright, it wasn't evening, and my gaze darted around for some awareness.

My buddy Jesse met my eyes.

His own eyes wide, concern worried his brow. "Colton?"

"What the hell happened?" I swallowed, holding my neck, then rubbing my chest. Sweat coated my fingertips, and the expanse of a large living room filled my vision, my house.

You're at home. You're home.

I sat up on the couch, pressing my palms to my eyes to alleviate the rush in my head, and Jesse sat beside me, hesitant. He leaned forward. "I was just trying to wake you up."

"With what?" I snipped, shooting him a look. Whatever he did, I couldn't breathe, and that wasn't in my head, not this time.

He picked up a pillow off the floor. "I shoved the corner up your nose. Like I always do to get your ass up?" He tossed it to the floor. "You sleep like a rock, Colt. You know that."

That was before. That was thirty days ago.

"I suppose that was a dick move of me... after what happened," he said, resting his arms on his knees. He touched my shoulder. "You okay? I didn't mean to freak you out."

Tilting my head, I didn't like the way my friend was looking at me, sympathetic and shit like I was broken. Sitting up, I punched his shoulder. "Nah, I'm good. I just overacted, I guess."

He watched me get up, stumbling a bit as I got my bearings.

He put a hand out. "You... You really okay, though?"

I found my phone as he asked, then cringed at a cracked cellphone screen. Pushing my hand over the scruff on my head, I turned, waving the phone.

He cringed back. "Shit. I fucked up. I'm sorry, Colt."

"It's cool. Cool," I said, taking a seat on the arm of my white leather sofa. I shrugged. "I'm the one who fell asleep with it, and yeah, I'm good. Just disoriented."

His chin went up. Leaning back, he folded his arms over the back of the couch. "What were you sleeping down here for anyway?"

"Damage control," I said, lifting the phone. "I pretty much talked to every member of my entire family last night." And went well into the morning doing it. The calls caught up with me after the press conference. I should have known the no missed calls were from my time in the air with no signal. Well, they all came in a wave at once, and I went down the line. The last had been my pop.

"If you want, we can come down," he'd said, gruff but sincere. That has always been his way. "Ann and I can plan a trip and leave tonight if you need it."

Ann was my stepmom, and the fact my old man was willing to travel all this way (when he hated flying) let me know the ringer I put my family through. One thing I appreciated about his call was his last words, though.

He'd said, "If you need it." He gave me an option, which hadn't been the welcome I got from my gram and aunt. I flat-out refused for them to come down here. I couldn't be around any of them right now—especially if they all came at once.

I feared suffocation if they did.

And anyway, my gram had her fill of watching me sick. She stayed with me that entire week before I was sentenced, and I couldn't go through that again. I couldn't go through *her going through* that again. Besides, I went to rehab, and that fixed everything as far as my entire family was concerned.

"The entire Chandler clan," Jesse said, letting a breath out with it when he threw his head back. "Rough."

The roughest. Jesse and I had been friends for a long time. We'd been drafted together, so of course, he knew the nature of my large family. I loved them, but they definitely could smother a guy sometimes.

I drew a hand down my face, shaking my head. "I ain't ready, man."

"I don't blame you. Look at your military ass." He shoved a hand down the back of my head. "Don't think the lack of hair will make you any faster than me on the court. I can still run laps up and down your blond ass."

He jostled me, and I snorted.

"Clean bill of health, remember?" I stated, placing my hand on my chest. "Served my thirty days, so I'm one hundred percent ready to kick *your ass*."

"And that's still bullshit," he went on. "That judge didn't know what he was talking about. You and I both know you aren't a drug addict."

One of the only ones that knew the truth. Jesse knew me. He knew me almost as well as I knew myself.

He chuckled. "If a guy can't have one night to get fucked

on his day in the sun, then what is the world coming to?" Reaching over, he gripped my hand, and I was almost glad he came over and tried to suffocate me. I hadn't felt normal at all since that day, but with him here, things started to feel that way a little bit.

He stood. "Come on. I need to raid your fridge."

Moments later, Jesse spread his arms, wrapping their length around the fluffy body of my housekeeper scrubbing down my kitchen counters. "Irene!"

She turned within them, squeezing the life out of him so hard he made a show of sticking out his tongue. "Jesse," she stated, her eyes warm, and her expression even warmer. The woman was always inviting and older, she'd come to work for me a few years ago. She'd been with this house even before that, another athlete.

Letting go, she squeezed Jesse's shoulders. "This house has missed you as much as Colton these last few weeks," she said, passing me a look over his shoulders.

I took a seat, grabbing an apple out of the ceramic bowl on the counter she'd stocked earlier in the week. "You've always been her favorite kid," I told him before crunching the fruit between my teeth.

Jesse simply shrugged, folding an arm over his chest. "Well, look at me?"

I kicked the back of his knee, making him stumble over himself with a chuckle.

Our childish banter had Irene looking offended. She placed her hands on her wide hips. "You know I play no favorites between you," she said, waving us off. "But I enjoy cooking your favorites. Can I make you something?"

"Nah," I told her, taking another bite. I spoke around the taste explosion. "Jesse is just going to clean me out."

"My housekeeper doesn't rock like yours." He'd already

dipped himself in my fridge, his ass wiggling in the air to his own internal beat, the idiot.

This made Irene smile. Jesse always knew how to hit that sweet spot with a woman, didn't matter the age. She patted my face. "Now, let me know if you need anything," she said, letting her fingers slip from my cheek. She turned. "You too, Jesse."

His arm rose above the chrome refrigerator. He'd found the beers—and well before 10:00 AM. Irene couldn't hide her distaste, but she let it go, sliding me a warm look before leaving the kitchen with her rag. She was another person that was still doing the kid gloves thing around me. I barely heard her around the place, and she could be in the same room as me, taking care of the house.

I was just glad she took off on the weekends, *that weekend*.

A trough of food hit my polished counter, Jesse the delivery boy. He proceeded in opening a carton of eggs, cracking open basically the entire stock in my food processor before grabbing the Muscle Milk. "Making you and me some energy," he said, grinning to himself over the sound. "We got to get as many workouts in as possible before you drop my ass like old news for Miami."

I smiled. My phone chirping took me by surprise and I moved my hip to reach for it, happy the damn thing was still in commission. But then, I saw the last person I had somehow managed to not talk to calling me this morning.

My brother Griffin.

He'd been quiet since I got back, too quiet, but I thanked the world for small favors. I wouldn't question it.

"Ironic you bring that up," I told Jesse. The phone stopped ringing and instead of calling back, I texted.

What's up? He had called me but a text was me being chicken shit. Jesse was looking at me when I gazed up and I lifted my shoulders. "Just got a call from Griffin. He's bugging me about something."

Jesse cringed, pouring our thick yellow beverages into a couple of mugs. "Yeah, what's going on with that? Him? Miami?"

I wished I knew. My fate was just as fuzzy as it had been... before the incident. I technically hadn't signed anything. Just had an offer. I placed my phone down. "Joe's set up a meeting with Miami but wouldn't give me much else than that. He gave me a date and time. That's it."

I got that text last night before I went to sleep, and I was surprised I *could* sleep with that weighing down my mind.

Placing the cups down, Jesse lounged back. He pushed one my way. "You think they'll bow out?"

God, I hoped not. It wasn't in the plan. *Miami* was the plan. I shook my head, watching my phone buzz.

Hey, Griff's text. *Not much. Just checking in.*

Of course he was. They *all* did. I typed letters behind a shattered smartphone screen. *Still here. Still breathing.*

And you know that's good to hear.

I breathed.

You mind some company? he asked, and I thought not him too, but then his text went on. *Roxie is coming into town. She has Jackson, and he wants to see his uncle.*

My thoughts and spirits lifted at the mention of the little tyke. Their son was three now. Jesus, how had that happened? I must have been getting old. I moved my hand over my head. *What are they doing here?*

Roxie is meeting with a client. She doesn't like leaving Jackson with the nannies if she's going to be gone for more than a couple days. Especially, if no one is going to be home. I'm out of town, too. In Texas, with Pop and Hayden.

Now, the optimist in me wanted to say he went home for business-related things, but the pessimist couldn't help but think he teamed up with our brother and dad to discuss *my issues*. He just said Pop and Hayden so maybe I could take the optimistic route. But still, this little visit with Roxie and my nephew sure was coming at a weird time.

This isn't an intervention, is it? I texted. *You letting Roxie come down and spread her magical powers of positivity and bringing my nephew as a buffer?*

He responded with, *LOL,* to that and his, *Hardly*, that followed let me at least know this conversation was different from the others I had with our family. I didn't know where Griffin and I stood since my incident. I could imagine he was disappointed just like the rest of our family though.

Jackson genuinely wants to come down and see you, he texted. *He's been asking about you.*

Probably because my name had been on so many lips lately. I was quite sure the word "Colton" was a buzzword for him.

Besides, Griffin continued. *You gotta help me work on his skills. Roxie ignores it, but the boy's talent is already showing on the court. I can't keep that mini basketball out of his hands. We set him up a hoop in his room.*

That made me smile, and him and my sister-in-law coming just might be the thing I needed to get my mood back up, if not a little. I told Griffin, *Sounds good,* surprised that Jesse managed to stay quiet during the entire exchange.

He sipped his drink, brown eyebrows raised above his cup.

"All good," I told him. "My sister-in-law is coming down on business. She's bringing my nephew with her."

"Hmm. When are they coming?"

That just came in via text, and my eyes widened, but only in surprise. They flew in today, arriving early afternoon, but that wasn't a problem. Work was extremely slow right now, and not just because of the obvious. The season had wrapped, so my days had been training and endorsement deals I had signed. The endorsements had stopped... but the training didn't have to, even if my future was undetermined.

Thinking I wanted to get that going, I grabbed Jesse's experimental drink, ready to go out and warm up the basketball court I made sure this house had before I bought it. A hand slamming down on my bicep made me choke on the already hard-to-get-down beverage, and I hacked, the eggs burning my nose. I held my bridge.

"Jess?" I shot, turning his way. "You trying to kill me?" First the damn pillow and then this? He wasn't responsive, staring out the glass overlook in the kitchen. It oversaw the entire back of my property from the second level, the grassy valleys of the Hills, but something told me he wasn't taking in the trees.

Ripples expanded into large liquid circles in my Olympic-sized pool, but soon enough, a head popped out of them. A body followed, shimmering and wet as it broke the surface.

Cami swam the length of the pool, her head rising and falling out of the water as she did some kind of stroke, and Jesse and I watched her. She did two entire full laps before pulling herself out of the water by the handrails.

Wide hips surfaced then, swaying with every step she took out of the pool. Two polished fingernails pushed into the bottoms of her bikini, sliding along the hem to adjust around two of the roundest globes.

Jesse sucked in a breath through his teeth. "That ain't Madison or Skylar," he said, watching Cami's ass move. Her back to us, she pushed her hands down a dark, wavy braid on her shoulder. Jesse squeezed *my* shoulder. "They're the only two you let stay the night. I still don't get how you juggle all these females."

I cringed at the statement, but even still, I couldn't take my eyes off Cami, moving in to get beside Jesse. She grabbed a towel now, dipping down...

I blinked. "We're not exclusive," I told him, referencing the two women he referred to, but he was right about one thing: they were the only women I let stay over. They were the only two who never made a thing of it and didn't go bragging to the press they were screwing a basketball player. For all intents and purposes, I was technically dating Madison and Skylar, *dating* and they both knew about each other so it wasn't a thing.

"And they both know that," I reminded him. "I'm not a pig."

"Yeah, yeah. Whatever," he said, waving me off. He hadn't blinked yet and surely wouldn't as Cami finished her towel's rotation over shapely legs, her skin toned and a rich copper brown. I never asked her, but assumed she was a mixture of races, and whatever they were left her more honeyed and golden than the best tan.

"Who is she?" Jesse continued, and it was like a switch went off. She was Cami.

She was Cami—my assistant.

"Christ," I breathed, grabbing his arm. "Get the fuck out of the window."

Jesse's eyes widened as I pulled at his t-shirt. "What the hell, Colt? What—"

But it was too late, as a set of deep brown eyes connected with ours, and even from this distance, how shocked they were was evident. Cami's mouth opening, I assumed a gasp fell from her lips that couldn't be heard because I was up here and she was down there. She shoved that towel against her front, fleeing the scene, and a fist went to Jesse's lips.

A bark of a laugh seeped out. "Holy shit! That was Cami? Colton, that was *Cami*? Holy shit!"

Holy shit was right, and the conversation she and I *just* had after I escorted her here from her apartment brewed to the surface.

"I'll keep out of your way," she'd said, being her ridiculous self. "But would it be too much trouble if I used your pool in the mornings? I usually swim at the YWCA."

I cut her off after that, knowing I paid her way too much money for her to be working out at the damn Y. I had chuckled then, telling her no problem, but even still, she wanted to work out a schedule for when she swam. In the end, she settled on 6:00 AM.

It must have been 6:00 AM.

∼

Cami

Yeah, this wasn't going to work, not at all, and the fact I currently didn't know the whereabouts of my purse made this whole thing just damn golden.

Find it. Find it, get your stuff, and get out.

But the thoughts proved to be a feat in themselves. I had at least five boxes of stuff, and the fact that the purse was missing in action made the concept of leaving even less of an option. I tore my room up, a beautiful one really. Colton put me up in one that overlooked the basketball and tennis courts. A luxurious garden view surrounded it.

Too bad it was all short-lived.

I ripped apart the bedroom, tossing sheets and throw pillows before thinking I might have left my purse in the closet. I'd been in there practically all night, organizing and unpacking the empty boxes, and that made me feel even more of a fool. One would think I was nesting with him or something when this arrangement was supposed to be temporary.

That had been your first mistake, saying yes.

There had been no reason to agree to all this. Yes, I needed a place to stay, and yes, he offered space at his home to me at no cost, but those had all been reasons to say no. Not only would I be staying here in this house, but I'd be staying with Colton—*my boss* Colton. He was my employer who I'd found in this very place, choking half naked in his own vomit. The images still burned and were a direct contrast to how he came at me yesterday. He'd been himself and seemingly normal, but he couldn't be, not after that.

He couldn't possibly be after... after...

I fell to the closet floor, chewing my lip. I needed to get out of here, but my purse clearly wasn't in the room. Odds were I left it on his kitchen counter or something. I did that at home all the time, but going downstairs wasn't an option. Not with him and Jesse Staring-All-Up-In-My-Business Michaels downstairs. Deciding to wait it out, I repacked up the closet, filling those boxes that should have never been emptied. That killed an hour or so before I decided to handle some *other* Colton business. Joe, his agent, had emailed me his list of events just this morning, and I hadn't gotten to that yet.

Mostly because the lack of planned events was disheartening. I assumed his schedule would go right back to what it had been after being cleared for thirty days. He lost so much because of what happened and probably hadn't even been told that. That was Joe's job I guess. Not mine.

After a couple hours, my gaze flickered to the elapsed time, and I groaned, snapping the laptop shut. This was dumb. I was going downstairs, getting my purse, and then would be telling Colton I'd find other arrangements. He'd understand. I stressed privacy and clearly didn't have that even after requesting I have access to the pool at a designated time. I had been more than reasonable about that too since it had been so early.

I got dressed after my shower and ended up choosing Capri khakis and low-heeled pumps before opening the bedroom door and slipping out of it. Sneaking down the marble-tiled hallway, I quickly realized the heels had been a lapse in judgment and slid them off. Colton didn't stay on this side of the house, but still. I wasn't trying to make a big deal of me leaving.

I found the kitchen easily, grateful Irene wasn't there and even more that Colton and Jesse were absent. Dear God, Jesse Michaels. I was sure I'd hear about the little "incident" at the pool soon enough from him. He loved giving me a hard time.

God, this was such a bad idea. And the frustrations loomed at a bare countertop. I gripped it, tapping my nails for a moment while I thought about the other places my purse could be.

A crash shot my back up.

My chin dipped at the sounds again, pots and pans, and I lowered, cracking open the counter doors. A pair of the chubbiest light brown cheeks shined rosy my way, dark eyes and a flourish of short amber curls above it all. The child who owned them gave a toothy grin with only a few teeth, giggling as he held... my missing handbag. He had its contents spilled out and, judging by the back of the counter door, had also been using my lipstick as a crayon. He'd scribbled illegible letters in red, the tube of MAC lipstick still balled up within his tiny fist.

I frowned. "There's a little person in here."

A baritone snort came from behind me as well as a body that went on for miles when I turned.

"Nice observation, Cami," Colton said, traipsing into the kitchen in a pair of black sneakers and shorts, and really, that's all he wore. His chest bare, he had a t-shirt in hand, beads of an undefinable liquid dotting a body bronzed in color. A fragrance lingering in the air, which was thick and only male, told me he'd come from the shower. His flushed cheeks and the slight rose tint to his skin only gave it away more.

I rose, silent, as he came around me, shrugging on that

shirt to cover his wide body. With a grin, he dipped and the child was in his arms. He tossed the boy over his shoulder and his little legs kicked, the most delightful sounds bursting out of him in gleeful wisps.

"You were supposed to be watching TV with Ms. Irene until I got out of the shower." Colton laughed, spinning with him.

"Irene! Irene!" He giggled, reaching, and Irene came into the kitchen, her hand on her chest.

"Little cutie pie, there you are," she said, pinching his cheeks. He slid over to her from Colton's arm and she swung him. "We were playing hide-and-seek," she cooed. "But this little one hides too well."

Colton fell back to the counter. "*I* could have told you that was a bad idea. The big guy is good at getting away when he doesn't want to be found," he said, grabbing him back. He blew one of those air bubbles people do on the boy's stomach before setting him down on his, what looked to be, tiny Air Jordan's. "As well as faking right and faking left," Colton continued, getting low with the child.

The kid jumped up and down, and the two proceeded to play a game of imaginary basketball, trying to get around each other. Colton squeaked across the tiles of the kitchen like he wasn't a massive guy in a tiny room, but yeah, the whole thing was kind of cute. Eventually, the little kid found an in, escaping Colton, but I didn't think that had anything to do with Colton not being able to handle the kid. He let him go, and the boy ran to play around Irene's legs.

Colton stood with a smile, and I couldn't help doing the same.

"Who is, um," I said, pointing in the general direction of the little boy. Last I checked, Colton had no kids I knew about.

Colton found me when he turned. "My nephew. Jackson."

But then his head lowered, and he chewed the inside of his lip. "Sorry. I would have told you he was coming, but didn't want to bother you. I figured you wouldn't want me to."

After this morning... that had probably been a good call, but still. I would have liked to be prepared. I mean, this was his house, but...

Yeah, this wasn't working out. Irene took Jackson by his hand, promising Colton he'd stay put this time. They left the pair of us in the kitchen, and the room felt super crowded despite only the two of us being in it. I busied myself, dipping to gather my purse.

"Damn," came from above me. "Sorry about that."

Colton's warm body was suddenly beside me. Reaching out, he slid the longest fingers around the smallest tube of lipstick. He handed it to me, and I grabbed it, pushing my hair behind my ear. "It's cool."

He nodded. "He likes to get into stuff sometimes. Nothing's ruined, right?"

"No harm done," I told him. Though, my tube of Ruby Woo might need refilled. I'd let it go, though. It wasn't a big deal. "When did he get here?" I asked.

Colton folded his hands. "Um, about an hour ago? Roxie dropped him off while Jesse and I were scrimmaging on the court. The two of us played with him for a bit before Jesse went home, and I hopped into the shower."

"Roxie?" I asked, my interest piquing. "Your sister-in-law?" I had seen her in passing. She and his brother Griffin, her husband, lived out in Miami so I didn't see them often, but of course, I had heard about them. I'd heard about her and her consulting business.

"Yeah," Colton went on. "They flew in so she could meet with a client. I'm hanging out with the little guy until she gets done."

"Awesome," I said, busying myself by shoving the rest of

my stuff into my purse. With my haste, Colton shot his hands out to help, probably figuring he should, but his hands were so big he bumped me at every turn.

His eyes creased with the smile on his lips. "Making this worse, aren't I?"

Rather stiffly, I shrugged him off. Things didn't use to be this way between us, so weird and awkward. I think he noticed it too but wouldn't say anything about it. He rose when I did and stood there as I pushed the purse's strap over my arm.

"Thanks for the help," I told him before turning, but his hand came out, not on me, but on the counter. He used it to get closer to me, sliding in until he found my eyes.

I looked up at him, and his smile had wiped away.

He sighed. "About this morning, Cami—"

"It's cool."

"No, it's not. You asked for something. You asked for time, and I forgot. I'm sorry."

It came time for me to sigh now, shifting. "I really appreciate the favor of letting me live here. I do, Colton, but..."

"Good, so there's no *but* then," he said, standing tall.

But there was a *but*, a massive one that filled this room to the brim, and I didn't think it had anything to do with this morning. Some giggles sounded, Jackson in the other room with Irene, and I couldn't help smiling. Colton did too, and I was reminded of how nice he looked when he did. His whole face lit up, those bright eyes.

He turned. "Come to lunch with me. We're meeting Roxie, Jackson and I. We can sit down and..." He lifted his shoulders, shrugging. "I don't know talk before she gets there."

Talk. Talk...

I couldn't help but wonder what that meant, but then again, maybe I didn't.

Five

COLTON

I WATCHED Cami carefully from across the restaurant table, her hair all up and a set of white pearls in her ears. I asked her to a casual lunch, and she dressed up like we were at the Four Seasons instead of this old dive. I mean, my nephew gauged his time between playing with my sunglasses and the broken pieces of crayon in the red cup on the table, so this place being casual went without saying. That was Cami, though. Always professional. She even had the gumption to pull out a notebook from her purse, tapping the pad under her nails as if to say: "Just in case."

She sat back in our corner booth, bobbing her head to her own internal beat. She'd probably gaze out the window to busy herself if she could, but we'd been moved to a section without windows.

Paparazzi. They'd been the reason and currently clustered outside. They spotted my Beamer a couple blocks down the road and followed us the rest of the way to the restaurant immediately. Normally, I didn't pay them any attention, but I wouldn't have them getting Jackson on camera, and I... also wanted to talk to Cami—in private and without shutters around us.

It seemed she wanted to talk first.

"So I have my organizer," she said, reaching into her handbag. She pulled her iPad out, flipping the cover open. "Joe sent me your schedule, and we can go over the highlights before you meet with him."

That sounded as much fun as doing my taxes. "This isn't a business meeting, Cami. It's just lunch, and you're not on the clock." She knew that too, but I imagine she couldn't help herself. Socially, we never hung out in any type of capacity outside of functions for me so this was... new.

"Right," she said, putting her device away. The waitress came, and Cami's lips blew a breath out like she'd been holding it.

"What can I get you dears?" she asked, giving me a way-too-wide grin and the eye-over to go with it. I'd be flattered if she wasn't pushing my gram's age.

I sat back, giving her my best smile anyway. "This little guy will have chicken," I said, putting my hand on Jackson's curly head. He moved on to chewing the crayons now, and I fished them out of his mouth. "Nuggets or tenders; whatever you got will be fine with a side of fries. And for me, I'll have whatever the lady ends up ordering."

Camille's eyes widened, her fingers falling down her menu. "What if you don't like what I get?"

After I got the crayon from Jackson, I smiled at her. "But what if I do?"

"But what if you don't? I don't need that kind of pressure."

I rolled my eyes at her, moving to slide the waitress another smile as I passed her my and Jackson's menus. "Whatever she is having, please." I faced Cami's frown. "And you know I eat everything."

Her lips went thin. She righted her menu and eventually found something to her liking. "Burger and fries," she said. "Hold the condiments. I'll add my own."

The woman took the menu, leaving us after waving at my nephew, and Cami dropped her hands on the table.

"See, that wasn't so bad," I told her, picking up a crayon to help Jackson shade in a tree on his coloring placemat. My gaze lifted to Cami, but her eyes were on anything but me.

She folded her arms over her chest. "I hate when you make me do that. Put me on the spot like that."

Because I guess I had a time or two, now that I thought about it, so she had been right about that, I supposed. I'd done it at business lunches or other social appearances for the job, but usually someone else was with us. Joe, Jesse, or sometimes a lady friend. In those situations, I just went along with what they ordered, opting to put my order in last.

Camille's cheeks filled with color after what she said, and she chose to stare at the wall instead of me. I really felt bad at the unintentional tension. I'd been feeling bad about that for a while now on what I used to consider an easygoing relationship.

You can fix that, though.

She spoke before I did. "When's Roxie joining us?"

"Um, should be any minute now," I told her, shrugging down in the booth for my phone from my pocket. Before we left the house, I had texted Roxie to let her know what place we'd settled on, and she confirmed she'd meet us while we were on the road. Thing was, I wouldn't let Cami use my sister-in-law as a crutch to avoid conversation with me.

Which was no doubt why she'd asked about her.

I put my phone down. "But like I said at the house, I wanted to talk to you first. Before she gets here?"

Deep brown eyes slid over. "You said that. About what?"

About everything. About what you saw...

I settled for something less heavy. "I wanted to thank you." I had her attention now. "For that night? I wanted to thank you for all you did. For saving my life."

Saying the words openly hadn't been as bad as I imagined. She had saved my life. She had been there... for me.

But then again, she always had, hadn't she? Cami. Perfect, put together Camille who always handled situations for me no matter how crappy or extremely minute they may be. She did things, *took action on things*, that went above and beyond her job title sometimes, and I never appreciated her like I should have. I didn't see her like I should have.

Well, I was seeing her now, sitting before me with her hands in her lap and lips parted. It was like she had words on them, but just couldn't form them.

Talk to me. Tell me what you have to say.

I wanted to pull them out of her and shake her to do it, hold her arms and squeeze ever so slightly. Her mouth opening kept me from doing that, her hand pushing a stray brown curl out of her eyes.

"Did it help?" she asked, shyly, and so *not* like Camille. "Did rehab help you?"

The question had surprised me, but it was an honest one. She, like anyone, might have that question for me, but Cami wasn't anyone. Cami was at the front lines of my life.

She wrote the press statement.

The soft coos of my nephew beside me sounded in the air. He sung to himself while he colored, and I just listened to him for a moment, trying to figure out everything I wanted to say. Eventually, I went with the script.

I opened and closed my hands on the table, smiling slightly. "Of course, but hey, you know that right? You wrote what I told the press."

Her face fell, her head down. Her tennis bracelet clinked

the table while she tapped her nails on it again. "Yeah, but, Colton—"

"Clean bill of health," I surmised, nodding my head with it. "My issue with drugs and excessive alcohol is cured."

Dark eyes found mine, reaching into my soul if at all possible. "But you don't have a drug problem, Colton."

The words shot through me and went deep, gripping on like a grapple hook. She really was on the front lines and, because of that, knew more than she probably should. She knew more than anybody probably should.

I guess that's why I decided to keep her close.

Well-seasoned, I passed what she said off once more with a slight wave of my head no matter how futile the attempt. "I guess some of us have ways of hiding our vices," I told her. *Our pain.*

That mouth of hers went thin again, and she leveled me a hard gaze that said more than any words could. "Yeah, I guess so," she said, then shifted her stare over the restaurant. That only left more tension between us, but again, that had never been her fault.

My saving grace came in the form of a woman in a business suit with a set of brightly colored eyes. My sister-in-law Roxie had a smile on her face and a wave for me when she spotted our corner both.

I rose up, standing.

"Sorry I'm late," Roxie said, wrapping a tiny arm around me. She had to pop up on her toes to get to me, her being so small and petite like Camille.

Where had *that* thought come from? I supposed I saw a little too much of my assistant this morning, so I blamed it on that. I hugged Roxie. "Nah, you're not late at all. We just ordered."

"Oh, good, good." Roxie had changed so much since I first met her years ago on my gram's ranch. She was all business and *mommified* now, but that wasn't a bad trait. Jackson exploded in his booster seat, screaming, "Momma, momma!" with an edge on it as thick as any accent from my oldest brother, Hayden's, kids. He had two girls.

Griffin must be rubbing off on the little guy.

Smiling wide, she grabbed her son, hugging him close as he wrapped his arms around her. "Was he good?" she asked, patting his back.

"Perfect," I said, maneuvering his booster seat out of our booth to give her room to sit with him on our side. I never had a bad thing to say about my nephew. He was super well-behaved. I didn't consider myself great with kids, but when it came to him, he made it all easy. My nieces? Yeah, they ran around like crazy kids. Cami watched our exchange. She'd stood, her hands clasped in front of herself, and I motioned her way. "Roxie, you remember Cami? My assistant?"

"Yes, of course," she said, giving her a hand over Jackson. "How have you been, Cami?"

And why did my assistant look thrown for a minute like she didn't have words at first? Again, so not Camille. Her head shook slightly. "Great, and you?"

Roxie shrugged, sliding into the booth with Jackson. The waitress brought a high chair, and he soon took up residence there. "Fine, though a little tired," she admitted with nothing but that sunshine she always gave off. "Quick trip, but successful trip."

"Oh, what are you working on?" Cami asked, leaning in. I wasn't surprised she got into business talk right away. That was just her.

"Just got done vetting a couple of sports agents. I like to meet them firsthand before I approve them to our lists. I think they'll make nice additions for our clientele."

What Roxie did for the sports community was really amazing, and no doubt saved many young players from what could be real sharks in this business, myself probably included in that number. She found Joe for me, and I couldn't be more appreciative of that. I considered that guy more than my sports agent, but my friend.

"The real work begins when I get home, though," Roxie continued. "I had to fire my marketing head recently. I hated to do it, but she kept flaking out on me. Calling in sick and *not* showing up for work sometimes."

Cami made a face. "How unprofessional."

Roxie nodded. "Yeah, it's put me in a spot with our plans to rebrand. We're trying to get new slogans and a revamped mission statement in place. I've always loved the old ones, but Griffin and I were talking and feel new ones will freshen up the brand."

My brother a businessman. So crazy to even think about that, but it was cool he found himself to be a dual threat with that and his sport.

"That sucks," I told Roxie. "About your marketing head?"

"Mmmhmm, but we'll figure it out, though."

Our little friend, the older waitress, came back, and Roxie gave her an order of a turkey sandwich on rye, and all the while Camille watched her, chewing her lip like she wanted to say something. I smiled then, a thought coming to my head. I waited until Roxie got done ordering, but then, I threw it out there.

"Camille can probably help you out," I told my sister-in-law, picking up my water to take a sip. I swallowed. "If not temporarily until you find someone. She's got a degree in marketing and communications from NYC."

Cami's lashes flashed to me as if surprised I knew that for some reason. Of course I knew that. She worked for me.

Roxie smiled at her. "Is that true?"

Now, I knew from moments previous Cami *loathed* being

put on the spot, but in that moment, no one could wipe the smile off her face.

Her shoulders lifted, going modest. "I used to work in corporate America for a while."

My eyes widened a bit at that, that one bit of news new to me. Cami had come to work for me through a hiring agency, and I knew about NYC as she'd told Joe in passing. I mean, it didn't surprise me at all really that corporate America was her background, and she herself made more sense a bit. How *together* she always seemed to be made sense, but what had me a little confused was her current position.

Working for me.

"So it wouldn't be a problem," Cami went on. "If you need the help, I can put something together. I just need to know what you're looking for."

"And you wouldn't mind letting her go for a bit?" Roxie asked, turning in her seat to me. "I mean, it would all be through email, but yeah, I'd love the help."

I offered her a smile, then Cami. Her eyes on me, she seemed to be looking for some type of approval, which I had no problem giving.

The two hammered out the details through the rest of lunch, shooting around a couple details or two, but I think they kept it at that since I was there. We had a pretty casual lunch, and I liked that whatever pressure had been there between Camille and me seemed to have evaporated. My sister-in-law being her usual ray of sunshine I was sure had something to do with that. After dessert came goodbyes, and we went out the back of the restaurant to do them. Gratefully, the paparazzi only thought to stalk the front of the dive.

Roxie gave me a hug with a sleeping little boy between us. Jackson was knocked the hell out before his ice cream even came.

"Thanks for watching him," she said to me, then waved to

Cami when she offered to take the leftovers to the car. "And thanks, Cami. I'll be sending you that email."

Cami's head lowered, nodding. She told me she'd be in the car, her arms filled with Styrofoam to-go containers.

"She's nice," Roxie continued, finding me over her shoulder.

"She's, um, she's something. Professional if not anything."

"Yeah," she said with a wide smile. Her hand pressed to Jackson's back, rubbing while we both watched the back restaurant traffic for a bit.

"She was there, right?" Roxie suddenly said, and I had to say I thought that question would come sooner. "That night, at your house?"

Pushing my hands into my jeans, I nodded. "She was. She saved my life."

"Mmm," came from her next, and I feared the follow-up, but then I wondered why.

She gave me a hug, my nephew between us. It said so much with absolutely no words at all. She didn't let go for a long time, and after it was over, she mentioned not one more word about the incident. She left it at that, taking Jackson with her after I said goodbye to him.

And she'd never know how much I truly appreciated that.

Six

CAMI

LUCKY, Tommy typed. His envious keystrokes followed up with several smiley faces, so I knew he did have some genuine happiness for me.

Grinning, I keyed, *Just working my way through this thing.*

Because that's all I had been doing for the past few years, trying to make my way and finally, *finally* getting my foot in the door of something worthwhile. That journey started with my move to Los Angeles. My job as an athlete's assistant had always been a means to an end, a jumping point for my career in a new environment.

It was one happily unknown to me.

Well, you're definitely doing it, Tommy entered into the chat screen. We'd started chatting originally so he could notify me he'd finish organizing Colton's charity vouchers. One thing about my boss was he was actually very giving. Colton donated to several nonprofit organizations every month, and Tommy and I handled keeping track of them. By that, I meant Tommy did, and I approved them.

Being first assistant had its perks.

Let me know if you need a second chair on your new project with Roxie, Tommy went on. He ended the statement with a winking smiley, and I rolled my eyes at his choice of words. Tommy had been pre-law once upon a time and still often found a way to feed me terms like "boiler plate language" among other things.

Will be all over that, I told him, my sarcasm ringing through the words. To lessen the blow, I shot him my own winking smiley.

It wasn't that I believed Tommy couldn't help me. In fact, quite the contrary. He was brilliant really, a little panicky but brilliant nonetheless. I knew because I hired him myself, but I didn't want too many seasoned chefs in the kitchen with this task. No, this project with Colton's sister-in-law? It was all mine.

Fine, spoilsport, he responded. *I'll try not to be green with envy as you work your way out of this place.*

As I work my way out...

I had only blinked and a small portion of my life went by. They'd been years of running, hustling.

They'd been years of Colton Chandler.

I'll bet you'll be happy to get out, Tommy went on. *When this project with Roxie leads to something?*

My fingers flicked to respond. They'd even hit a few keys, but I thought better of it, backspacing. My time working for Colton had been a difficult one to define and really hammer down if I had liked the time spent or not. I mean, it had been more than stressful, trying. In many ways, he fit the cliché of a standard young athlete. He was rich with fancy cars and wild parties. Then, there were the women who flowed through his life. God, so many women. I even juggled them sometimes, herding them like cattle around for the prince himself. But the thing about Colton was that side of him was only one. He gave the world a face, then went home with another. He had always been kind to me, fair, so that made gauging who he really was quite hard. He wore them both equally well, those two sides, and because he did, falling into an easy stride with him had been easy. I was *comfortable* with him in the sense that I knew how to handle him.

That was until recently.

I told Tommy I had to go, but thanked him once again for providing the charity spreadsheets. He really was an excellent boy Friday for me.

After closing out the chat box, I brought up Roxie's email. I had read it several times, but studied the content to make sure I noted every detail she needed for her vision of a rebrand for her company. She was very thorough so that made it easy, and my brain pulled for all the tips and tricks I learned on how to hook a buy through only so many words. I had been surprised to see the correspondence so quickly in my inbox. Roxie's message had come in a couple hours after Colton had driven us back home, and that only made me respect her more for her ability to juggle the way she did. With her son, she no doubt played patty cake with one hand while drafting this email to me with the other, and she was in transit too. At lunch, she said she planned to be back in Miami to make a meeting she had with a client the following morning. Working woman, mom, she was like Super Girl, and I had so much respect for that. I aspired to *be* that one day.

I worked hard on the project, burning the midnight oil. Eleven o'clock saw me getting a cup of coffee, one I snuck out to a drive-thru to get. I didn't want to root around Colton's house more than I had to do so. I had been grateful for Colton sharing Roxie's opportunity with me, but I couldn't ignore the elephant in the house between us if I ran into him.

"Clean bill of health," he'd said at the diner, and also, "You wrote what I told the press."

I had written his press statement, which made it all so much worse. I thought just earlier that Colton had always been fair to me, and I *believed* he never made me uncomfortable or do anything I didn't want to do, but that wasn't entirely true. He had made me do something I didn't want to do. He had me lie for him.

I wonder for how long.

The heat behind my fingers burned me out of my thoughts. I placed my coffee cup on the counter, shaking my hand out before sucking on the red welts on my fingertips. I needed to finish this project so I could ultimately leave. It was time to start converting my position to something less intense and less stressful.

Nodding to myself with the thought, I went to pick up my cup in the kitchen warmed only by evening light. A gasp caused me to turn my head. Facing the hallway, I stepped toward it. The gasp hit again, and I padded that way, turning my head while I rounded the corner. But then I heard something only in my dreams, my nightmares.

A voice called out, deep and so much pain lined the surface. I sped toward the voice, fear in my veins.

Oh, God, please not again.

My hands to my lips, my entire body shook as I came across a familiar scene. Colton. He lay on his white leather couch, blankets wrapped around him every which way. Fortunately, that's where the familiarity ended. He didn't thrash tonight, but merely stirred. His arm went over his eyes, and a croak left his lips this time. He was having a dream, most likely a nightmare like I believed I'd come across when I fled to this room.

His arm fell, and his head popped up, his chin in the air like he was trying to rip out of himself or whatever he suffered from behind his eyes.

I ventured to the couch, not knowing what to do. Were you supposed to wake people up when they had a bad dream? Or maybe that was just when they were sleepwalking.

I took the edge of the couch, just enough room for me to sit beside him. "Colton?"

No response came from him, his head turning. His eyes creased as he panted, and I couldn't take it anymore, seeing him that way. I put my hand on his shoulder before I could stop myself. I needed to shake him, make this all stop or something. Almost immediately, a hand shot out toward my wrist.

His fingers gripped me so tight but then, eventually, loosened up. *He* loosened up, along with the rest of his body.

My hand coasted, the pads of my fingers traveling the line of his shoulder bone. He had such strong shoulders, and all the while he held me. He held me as I made it to his neck. With his short buzz cut, his hair was rough at the nape. My fingers stayed there.

He opened his eyes then, and his curly blond lashes reminded me of the head of hair he used to have. I didn't miss it, though. I liked him this way.

Blue eyes shifted but found mine quickly. He blinked. "Cami?"

I went to let go of him, and the awareness of our hands came to him. He let go, and I took my hand back, placing it in my lap. "You were calling out," I told him. "In your sleep?"

His lashes lowered slowly over his eyes. He pressed palms to them as he sat up. "Thanks," he said, drawing his hands down his face. "For waking me."

I nodded, giving him room as I slid to the other end of the couch. "Why are you sleeping down here and not upstairs?" It was late. He should be in his bed.

Reaching over, he touched the lamp on the end table. The room filled with soft light, and the space of a champion lit the room. His trophies were everywhere, the accomplishments decorating the back wall behind his entertainment stand. He'd done so much in only a few years in his field.

"I haven't since that night," he admitted, staring at his

legacy too. Maybe because I was. He dampened his lips. "Just haven't."

I pushed my leg under my knee. Normally, I might have been concerned by my appearance, oversized t-shirt and bed shorts. I worked all night and wanted to be comfortable, and Colton wore something similar, his long body in shorts and a ribbed tank top.

What he'd said had me more concerned.

He had admitted something to me. He admitted something I had no idea he wore on his person, considering how he'd been acting since he got back.

And so went those different sides about him again.

He ran a hand over his head. Maybe this wasn't my place, but my God, when had anything about him recently been my place?

"Does it happen a lot?" I asked, swallowing. "The nightmares."

He faced me, blinking once over bright eyes. "Every night."

He stared away after that, leaving me with that and nothing else. I wanted to tell him I had nightmares sometimes too. I wanted to tell him he'd made it into my dreams more than I woke up allowing myself to admit. Especially that first week after it happened. I fell into myself in the end, staying silent. We both did, despite how many words were no doubt unspoken between us.

Pressing his hands on his knees, he got up, and I frowned.

My legs lowered to the floor. "Where are you going?"

He turned. "Bed."

I stood. "But you just said you don't sleep there. You don't..." I breathed hard, choosing to continue. "You don't have to go up because of me. Look, I'll leave."

A hand went around my forearm, sliding to my wrist.

"Stay," he whispered, drawing me back *close* to him. "Stay, and I'll stay too."

Colton put off a heat, a warm one I felt inside and everywhere around. He sat on the couch, and I sat too, beside him instead of on the other side of the sofa.

His fingers left my wrist and returned to his lap. "What were you doing up? It wasn't me... was it?"

I shook my head. "Working on that campaign for Roxie. It's coming along."

That made him smile for the first time tonight. "No doubt with you."

For some reason, what he'd said had me feeling shy. Maybe it was that striking flare of blue always looking at me.

"You're one of the hardest workers I've ever known," he said facing me. "Putting up with me."

It hadn't been easy. Especially as of late. Maybe he saw that in my eyes in the end, his lengthy blond lashes shifting away. Turning, he picked up the remote, promptly filling the moment with ESPN and Sport's Center.

"If I'm staying up with you, I'm not watching this," I said to him, casually taking the remote away. "I can deal with a lot of things, but sweaty boys fighting over a ball I can pass on. I get that enough with my day job."

His deep chuckle filled the room. "Go for it."

He'd keep me here forever if I let him, that stare of his entirely too intense. He was a distraction more than I liked, and I honestly didn't hear the moans on the television until Colton faced them, breaking me from the trance I'd been in. It seemed I saved myself from Sport's Center considering what was on the TV.

Oh, my—

Flustered, the dance my hands did with the remote resulted in no actual productive action. It only ceased execution of turning the channel and made my cheeks burn in front of my boss.

My boss who I accidentally played a reel of porn for.

The throws and passion of *Skinamax* were on full display, and fumbling, I clicked at the screen but to no avail, and Colton... well, needless to say, he was losing it beside me.

Laughter roaring, he was obviously aware he had these channels. These were his channels, but something about me coming across them brought the humor out of him like nothing else. He couldn't stop laughing and, eventually, saved me from myself when he acquired the remote. He clicked away the images of a man going down on a woman while he jerked himself off, but that didn't mean he let the topic go.

His silence left too quickly.

"You know, I figured when you said you didn't want to see a bunch of sweaty guys playing with balls that statement covered something like that as well," he said, his grin wiry. "But maybe I was mistaken? If so, that's okay. No judgment."

Angry at myself for actually choosing to stay down here with him when I should have been upstairs working on my project for Roxie, I got up. I made it maybe two feet before Colton shot out that extended length of his arm and secured my wrist.

He pulled me back to sit. "Cami, stop. I was just giving you a hard time. It's okay if that bothers you. Porn?"

"It doesn't bother me."

"It bothered you a little."

I frowned, which made his chest bump in laughter again. He turned off the TV completely, and tossing the remote on his coffee table, he tilted his head at me.

"It was just a little sex," he said, draping his long arm behind the couch. "Nothing to be weird about. People do it all the time."

Technically, he was completely right in his statements, but him saying it did make it weird.

And me listening made it even weirder.

Especially, since I didn't move right away, like I was waiting for him to say or maybe do something. I didn't like that, and I stood, shifting on my feet.

"All watching stuff like that does is skew your perceptions," I said, moving away from the couch. "Women don't come like that, and if they do, they're lying to you. Most don't at all. Let alone—"

My heart raced, my body frozen.

Especially by the look in his eyes.

His arm dropping from the sofa, Colton stared at me. Like he didn't understand what I said, or maybe he did but just didn't know what to say.

I mean, what could he say to that?

I couldn't fill in the blanks for him, and I didn't want to, having enough of this conversation. It never should have happened in the first place, and when I turned, I didn't stop because Colton grabbed me this time.

It was because he got behind me.

Standing, his extensive height cloaked the carpet ahead of me, his heat full on and hovering only inches from my body. He shouldn't be this close, but he was.

He brought me closer by my shoulder.

"Cami," he said, my name filled with something I shouldn't tolerate or accept. I shouldn't like it.

I shouldn't go fluid for it.

But I was, falling back as he gained. He leaned in, and when he did, that flourish of heat traveled directly down my spine.

"Cami," he said again, a whisper this time. His large fingers braced my side. "Have you never... has a guy never *done* that for you?"

I opened my hooded eyes. For a moment, I forgot what this conversation was about.

And where it came from to get to this point.

He was asking me questions I didn't want to be asked and making me recall things that were painful to recall. No, a guy hadn't done that for me. No, I hadn't experienced... pleasure the way most women had, but it wasn't for lack of experience.

It was lack of kindness.

That all came many miles and minutes before him, and I didn't want to explain it to him. I attempted to move, but once again, he didn't let me. Like he couldn't, like I couldn't let him either.

Instead, I chose to stand there, his hands on me, and when he leaned in this time, I didn't fight.

I only gave into it.

I gave into his hand going down my arm and his body that pulsed hardness right into mine. Capturing me by the shoulders, he hiked me up against him, his erection full on and surging into my lower back. He was feeling this too.

He was feeling *me* too.

My eyes shut tight as he rocked my body into himself. Breathing me in, he pressed firm hands to my shoulders.

"Can I touch you, Cami?" he asked, a desperation in his voice that pulsed a sudden want into my core. His nose grazed my earlobe. "Can I touch you and do that for you? It doesn't have to mean anything if... well, if you don't want it to."

He was giving me an out, a way to make this work without jeopardizing my relationship with him. But the thing is, it'd been rocky as of late. Things had been inappropriate, and him putting his hands on me now only pushed that. Knowing all that, I took his hand.

And placed it between my legs.

The very action made his cock jump against my back, his shallow breaths humming a trail down my earlobe as he escaped my hand and slid his beneath the hem of my sleep shorts.

Oh... God.

And really, that's all I could think, Colton's hands on me, his fingers dancing across tendrils of tiny hairs. I hadn't shaved in a while, but he didn't seem to mind, his digits sliding between my pussy lips and playing with my juices.

"You're so wet, Cami," he breathed deep, squeezing my shoulder. "You're so wet for me."

I was wet *because* of him, and I think by the awe in his voice he knew that. He was bringing something out of me, making me feel things.

"Can I taste you?"

I dripped around him at the words, my lower lips tingling as he played. Somewhere in the depths of my delirium, I felt myself nod, and when he turned me around, I believed he might push his fingers into his mouth like the guys often did in the dirty films on his TV. I never thought in a million years that'd do anything for me. It hadn't before.

But seeing this man and the way he stared at me... I'd definitely like it if he did. He chose not to in the end, and his heated gaze traveled the length of me, stopping on my pussy before he took my hand. He guided me to the couch, told me to sit.

Then turned the lights off.

One touch of his table lamp, and nothing but the moonlight coming in through his giant windows brightened the area. His couch sunk down when he put the entirety of his weight on it, and grabbing the back of my thighs, he pulled me closer.

My panties and shorts came off next.

He got a big fist full of them, tugging them down my hips, then off in a single action.

"Open your legs," he said, his erection bulging through his

shorts. He ran a hand over his buzzed head as he watched me ease my legs apart. "Wider."

My bud pulsing, I spread my legs as wide as I could, my knee knocking the back of the couch. Even still, this didn't seem wide enough for Colton. His large hands braced my legs, exposing me more, and after he pinned my legs down, he sat back on his haunches.

He dampened his fingers.

One, then two he pushed into his mouth and down his tongue, but not the pair that'd toyed with me earlier. He used the other two, leaning over me.

"You're going to taste so good," he said, priming me as he spread my lower lips. He slid over my bud easily, making it pulse between his two fingers and his thumb.

Especially when he pinched.

Jesus!

"Don't for call Jesus, baby. Call for me," he said alerting me that the word escaped my lips just as easily as I thought it. He pinched again, and when I squirmed, he forced me to rock my hips into what we were doing.

"Feel it," he said sounding so Texan with his lazy drawl. I caught it too when he told me to call out for him.

When he called me "baby."

I allowed myself to forget that word, because if I didn't, I might tell him to stop. If I didn't, I might regain my senses and call this whole thing off, and I totally should. Colton was my boss and—

"Cami, I'm losing you," he said, making my eyes focus on him, and when he leaned over, I thought he might kiss me.

Instead, he went right between my legs.

Kisses light, tender, they acted as if they were loving me above instead of below, Colton's tongue easing out and pushing my lips apart. He sucked, stroked, and soon, I was gripping the back of his head in ways that made me grind my hips.

"That's it," he groaned, cupping his hand over mine. "Guide me to what you need."

What I need...

No one had ever done that for me, said that to me, but here he was, his mouth on me as he told me to tell him what to do. He told me to tell him what I needed through my body, and we weren't even in a relationship together. We were just two people, one working for the other.

But that's how it always started, isn't it?

I let those images of another time fade away, trying to do this, stay with this man between my legs who was making me feel so good. He was making me feel so wanted and desired in every way. I didn't know why this was happening or why Colton was doing this, but being honest, I couldn't make myself stop him. I simply drove my hips into his face, letting him eat me out from the inside as he gave me the best pleasure I'd ever felt in my whole life. His tongue entered me, and he took me on a new playing field, sucking me dry, and when he squeezed my clit with two fingers, I knew I was close.

"Cami..."

He said my name as my body spasmed, his fingers releasing my bud to grab my thighs. Strong, he held me to his mouth, not allowing me to escape. His tongue traced my opening, and when he dipped his tongue in, I knew he was getting that full taste he desired. He brought me to my peak.

He made me come.

I believe I had before, but really, anytime before this moment I didn't recall. It'd never been memorable enough.

It'd never been this.

I relaxed on his mouth, and at the same time, he massaged the back of my thighs, letting me fall away into another place. It was the euphoric place of him and what he'd done, his hands sliding up my hips and to my waist. Rising, he had the look of a man just as sated as I felt, his large arm wiping across his mouth. He was hypnotic, a force of a man between my open legs.

"Colton—"

He kissed my forehead instead of my mouth and when he eased himself to the back of the couch, pulling me with him, I realized something. That'd been the only kiss he had given me, on my forehead and nothing more. He braced me to him from behind, spooning me, and the hardness pressed into my bottom, let me know he wasn't going to ask for any more. He just wanted me to come.

He wanted to do that for me.

Seven

CAMI

"Colton?"

I snuggled close to the blanket he placed on me sometime during the night, my big curls in a halo around my head when I rose from the couch. I grabbed my skull, and a fury of all that happened last night filled my brain.

I can't believe we did that.

But we did, and dare I say it'd been... nice, more than nice. Colton's hands on me had felt amazing, his mouth even better, and raising my knees, I wrapped my arms around them. I stared out at the trees sprinkling the Hills beyond his window. The morning sun hit them perfectly. Where he lived was so breathtakingly beautiful it actually captured my breath.

What are you doing...

I didn't know. I worked here. Well, kinda. I worked for the guy who lived here, and the reality of that came crashing down on me. Colton was missing for some reason. I had no idea when he left, but there were some things that were hard to ignore. His arms around me felt like a large sense of home, and judging by how he'd slept so soundly last night, I hadn't been the only one that felt that way.

Steady, heated breaths tickled my earlobe last night, his body warm but most of all unshaken. He slept amazing, and though I didn't quite know when he left since I slept so great as well, I would wager to say *he* slept nearly the whole night.

I pressed my fingers to my lips. He hadn't kissed me, but I desperately wanted him to. I pressed my hands to my eyes, trying to force the thoughts and desires out. This couldn't happen.

I couldn't do this to myself again.

Taking the blanket off my lap, I quickly brought it back when I realized how naked I was under there. My curls whipping around, I didn't have to search long to find my undergarments.

They were folded right on the coffee table.

My heart squeezing at that, I brought them to me, then did one of those maneuvers to get dressed with a blanket over my lap. It wasn't like he hadn't had his fill last night, but Colton might be more levelheaded than he was before. I mean, I was, but then again, I wasn't so sure about that either. When I got to my feet, the excitement of seeing him actually made my heart race. This was something I hadn't experienced in a long time and definitely not since moving here.

I searched the house, putting my hair back up with an extra band I kept around my wrist. Searching the house was fairly easy considering I knew all the places he hung out, and when I came across the kitchen, I figured I found him from the sound of banging pans.

"Colton—?"

"Cami, sweetheart," his housekeeper, Irene, crooned, grinning at me as I came in across the linoleum tiles. The curvy woman got up from her position under the kitchen sink. "How's it going? I miss our Spanish lessons."

My Spanish was definitely rusty, but the woman had enlisted me to help her with a few words. She was headed to

Spain later this year with her family for vacation and asked for my help, but *again*, I was more than rusty.

My *abuela* would roll over in her grave if she knew.

"Too much of her father in her," she'd say and *not* in English. She loved my papa, a strong African American male, but she did feel he severely westernized my second-generation Mexican mother. It was something she and my father quibbled over all the time in even her final days of old age, but there'd always been love there.

"Oh, I do too. We'll definitely have to get back to it," I said to her, but silently hoped she'd forget. I was pretty busy these days and wasn't great at my Spanish. I smiled at her. "And I've been good. Just looking for Colton. Have you seen him?"

"I believe he's upstairs showering," she said to me, bending down to get another pan. She came up with a big baking sheet. "I hope I didn't bother you since you were on the couch."

Freezing, I forgot she lived here. Had she seen or... heard what went on last night? I mean, I didn't watch myself, but I knew I hadn't been quiet. I couldn't have.

He made me feel so damn good.

Recalling those thoughts and the possibly of her seeing or hearing us, my cheeks burned, but then, I realized today was Monday and she was probably just arriving this morning to start work.

Oh, thank God.

I breathed out heavy in relief, but composed myself.

"You're okay with where you're staying in the house, right?" she asked, knowing why I was here and everything. I mean, me staying here was house news, and as she ran the house, of course she knew. "I just ask since you were on the couch."

Her words cemented that she really wasn't privy to what went on, and I smiled at her, shaking my head.

"It's fine," I said. "I was just up working late last night. Went out for some coffee."

"I saw that too," she said getting another pan. "It must not have been very good."

"Why do you say that?"

"Because it was full," she said, tossing a smile over her shoulder. She rose up from the floor again. "I disposed of it this morning when I found it."

Nothing short of dread filled me, and with a coy smile, Irene went back to what she was doing.

"I'm getting these pans out for Colton," she said as I backed to flee the room. "He said he wanted to make breakfast this morning."

I froze full stop, and when I turned, Irene's wide smile was on me.

"I'm happy you're staying with us, Cami," she said, her brown eyes big and bright. "It's good for this house, good for Colton."

Her look almost seemed knowing on me. She lowered back below the sink, closing those cabinets. I didn't know what to feel about what she said, what she might know, but it all surrounded what I initially felt when I got up this morning. I woke up alone...

And how I wished I hadn't.

It was all madness, insanity, and when I scaled the steps up to Colton's room, I didn't knock first in my busy thoughts. I should have knocked.

Because there was a naked girl in there.

She rose up from the sheets the moment the door blew open, the scene too familiar, and my chest caved.

"Cami?" she questioned, sleep clearly in the woman's eyes. A flourish of wispy, blond strands covered her shoulders and breasts. That's how I knew she was bare.

Her hair was the only thing that covered her boobs.

Realizing that, she brought the sheets up and I realized *I* knew her too. Well, at least knew of her as I wrangled Colton's harem from day to day. Skylar Daniels was one of the few women he actually let stay over in his house, and it wouldn't be uncommon to find her here and half dressed whenever I came over to get Colton's ass up for a day of work. She made her way around the house all the time, and Irene must have let her in.

Or Colton last night.

Like I said, I didn't know when he left, left me.

"What are you—"

"Sorry," I said to Colton's clear guest. I mean, she *was* in his bed. I backed away. "I was just looking for Colton."

"Oh, Colt's taking a shower," she said, *"Colt"* when she pushed that bush of big blond hair out of her face and pointed toward his bathroom. The door open, heavy steam pushed into the wide room. I hadn't noticed that when I came in.

Yeah, he definitely knew she was here.

The thoughts should hurt more, but I think, if anything, they released me from other thoughts that shouldn't have surfaced. They were impractical and the exact opposite from what I actually wanted. I didn't want to get in a relationship with my boss.

I didn't want to be hurt again.

I left the room without saying anything.

"I'll tell him you came by," Skylar tossed from behind me, but I didn't need her to do that for me. I didn't need anything from her.

I especially didn't need anything from him.

Eight

COLTON

"Cami?"

I scoured the house, it was curiously... vacant. Unusually, my sheets had been tossed when I got out of the shower. Like someone had been there waiting for me, and I *thought* it might have been her, Cami.

The reason I'd been in the shower for over an hour.

Her tight little bottom pressed up against me all night and into the morning, her body warm, and between that and the blue balls I gave myself, I needed some relief. Dick in hand, I jerked off to the memory of her sweet heat flooding my mouth, and I had to after what happened last night. She gave herself to me.

She let me make her come.

I couldn't believe she'd never had that experience, that a man either had never been able to or had the desire to actually do that for her. The latter maddened me, and I might have overstepped my boundaries when it came to her, but I hadn't cared. The desire to please her, have her overcame me, and I lost control of myself. I did something I probably shouldn't have, and what made it worse was I not only wanted to do it again, but finish the job I started last night. I wanted to see her in my bed this morning.

I wanted to make her come again.

Last night hadn't been about me, but this morning selfishness swarmed me, as I made my way through the house, checking all rooms. I told Cami things could be casual, but I at least wanted to talk about what happened. I figured we could discuss it over breakfast or something. Problem was, I couldn't seem to find her, and the pans I requested to start that breakfast were currently being put away.

My housekeeper banged and crashed pots and pans like she was trying to start her own percussion line when I entered the kitchen, and I caught a skillet just before she raised her little feet off the floor to hook it above the sink.

"I said I wanted to make the house breakfast," I said to her, and Irene had looked pleased when I offered. She didn't so much now when she got to her feet, and wiping her hands on her apron, she frowned at me.

"I'm afraid there's too much work for me to join you this morning, Colton," she said, standing back. "But I'm sure you can manage in the kitchen?"

Because I could, I nodded, but when she started to walk away I hadn't been quite done.

I clasped her arm. "Have you seen Cami? I can't seem to find her anywhere."

Though her physical presence appeared to be gone, her essence actually lingered in the air—especially, after last night. This might have all just been in my head, but I could feel her around me as if she'd been here. She'd really gotten to me like nothing else, and I really, really needed to talk to her.

Irene slid away. "Camille left for the day, Colton. And I'd mind you to keep better track of your company."

Frowning, I didn't understand what she said, putting the pan on the counter.

"Cami's staying here, Irene. She can come and go as she pleases—"

"I don't mean Cami, Colton," she said, her fluffy bangs brushing against her forehead before she pushed them back. "I mean, your guest. Ms. Skylar."

"Skylar?" My head shot back. "Why are you talking about Skylar? She isn't here."

"She was," she said, putting another pan away. "I told her to wait in the parlor for you, but I have a feeling impatience sent her upstairs to see you. She dropped by as she had a few minutes before work, but they must have not been enough to wait for you to finish upstairs. She said to tell you hello before leaving several moments ago, and Camille, well, she left only moments before that."

Moments before that...

"I have a feeling they may have intercepted each other," Irene stated, but I was already fishing my phone out of my pocket. I got another Irene frown. "Again, I say do better with your company, Colton. You're better than that."

A basket of laundry slid across the counter with her final statement, and though I obviously hadn't mentioned what went on with Camille, I was sure Irene had seen us together on the couch. She may have even encouraged it when she put an extra blanket on us. I'd folded it and returned it to the back of the sofa when I got up.

What the fuck did I do?

Dialing, I bypassed an incoming text. I didn't know who it was from, but I wasn't concerned. I was aiming for Cami's ears and went straight for them when I dialed her.

I knew exactly what I'd done as I listened to the phone ring. In my openness to allow one of the girls I was seeing to drop by whenever they damn well liked for a screw amongst other things, I let someone else get caught in the crossfire. But that someone wasn't just anyone. It was Cami, and though she knew the gory details when it came to my life, she should have never fallen into the rough of it. She didn't deserve that and definitely didn't deserve what she thought she saw.

Hi, this is Cami, personal assistant to Colton Chandler. If you need to leave a message for him or me please do so at the—

Hanging up the phone, I decided to text.

Hey. I ran into Irene. She told me you left. Please let me explain. It's not what you think with Skylar.

I left two more messages in the same vein before grabbing my car keys and heading down the hall to grab my shoes. Pressing my phone to my ear, I attempted a second call while I got them on but must have answered the phone with my cheek because my agent's voice was suddenly in my ear.

"Colt—"

"Sorry, Joe. This isn't a good time," I said stomping my foot down into one shoe before putting on the other. "I'm looking for Cami."

"Cami's here, son. But where are you?"

Confused, I placed both feet on the floor. "Wait. What? What do you mean Cami's with you? Where are you? Where's she?"

In the background, I heard male voices, Joe's amongst them, and when he returned, a sigh was in his voice.

"We were supposed to go over your contract stuff today, Colton."

My eyes closed, the reality of what he said coursing through my veins.

That was today...

"That's today," I concluded, knowing he'd scheduled me a meeting. He confirmed the time with me already.

"Colton..." And I didn't like how Joe said it, his voice something I'd heard before. It came after the initial shock of me almost dying. I hated this man's sympathy, someone I'd come to look up to over our time working together. I hated his disappointment even more. It'd become something of a normal occurrence when interacting with the people in my life as of late.

I only added Cami to the stack.

"Get here," Joe said, sighing again. "Just get here."

Nine

COLTON

Looking for Cami wasn't something I meant to do upon crossing the threshold of my agent's office suite, but something I instinctively did. My assistant was in my mind with no possible means to escape, and I just needed a few moments with her, to explain, but Joe got to me first. He found me lingering in the lobby, his hands up.

"Miami's here," he said, placing them on me. "You all right? Is your head here?"

Meaning was I... stable. Though he didn't actually say that. In the back of my mind I wondered if he questioned my mental state just as much as the rest of the world seemed to as of late. He believed the judge's sentence regarding my drug and alcohol use was just as much bullshit as I did.

But that didn't mean he didn't question the behaviors surrounding the actual act. He'd never say anything of course, but I didn't believe he had to. I saw it all over his face when he looked at me, handling me with kid gloves, as he shook my shoulders before pulling away. Guiding me toward his personal conference room, I allowed my gaze to travel again, looking for Cami.

I only found my brother.

I could actually see his big-ass grin from here, toothy and bright from all those tubes of Colgate I was sure he got for free for being one of their spokespeople. There wasn't a week that didn't pass without seeing my brother Griffin's face on an ad or a commercial since he went pro and even more frequently over the years as he settled into his stride. Griffin had become something of a legend even here in LA where I played. What I didn't understand was why he was here now.

Honestly, I didn't know how I would react upon seeing any of my family after my, well, after all I'd been going through. I strategically restricted all contact with them to either phone calls or text messages. My brother Griff was the first person I technically saw since getting out of rehab.

And something made it easier to breathe now that he was here.

I didn't understand that feeling as he rose from his seat, coming over to me. Broader, he had a width to his shoulders where I was narrower and a height to his frame that I just barely surpassed. I'd grown taller than him years ago, taller than all my brothers in the end. I supposed it'd been the one thing I had of my own being surrounded by nothing but rowdy siblings. They gave me a hard time being the youngest.

"Colton."

But they always protected me.

I felt that as my brother brought his extended limbs around me, his flaxen hair pushed back and making my new look resemble a kid's style. His pressed suit only pushed that distinction more. I came today in a popped-collar polo and dress pants. I was his baby brother in every way.

"Griff, what are you doing here?"

Emotion in my voice I didn't anticipate, I didn't let him go immediately. Eventually, he did draw back though and gripped the back of my neck. He took me in, smiling at me.

Griffin and I had always been the closest growing up. I figured that had to do with our ages. The pair of us were the youngest out of the four Chandler boys, and everything he seemed to touch I wanted to as well. I admired him I guess, my big brother. Taking my shoulder, my brother stood before me. Like I said, looking way better than me. He matured so much in what seemed like only a few years, and I figured I would be on that same path as well.

At least I had been.

His hand coming down, Griffin slid both into his pockets. "It's a big day for you," he said, tilting his head. "I guess I wanted to give my support."

I had no idea what that meant, and the possibilities didn't sit well. Especially as Miami seemed to be behind him.

Men I had met before reached to shake my hand, Miami reps and some of the most powerful men in the industry. The last time I'd seen these fellas we'd been having drinks, celebrating.

How much things had changed.

"Griffin's with us today, Colton," one of them said, the man in a fitted suit even fancier than my brother's. He settled a hand on top of mine. "We're all hoping to have some thorough discussions today."

Words like support and discussions really didn't sit well. There certainly hadn't been anything that needed supporting the last time I'd seen these guys, the decisions settled and the offers made. The men had me sit on one side of the table while they took the other, Joe on my side. Griffin joined the men, technically his reps still, I supposed. We all squeezed in, and Joe took the lead.

"Colton apologizes for being late, gentlemen," he said, shaking my shoulder like I was two. I supposed I acted like it, considering my tardiness for such an important meeting. My agent smiled at the group. "But he's here now, and he's ready to talk."

"And we're ready to both engage and listen," said one of them, his nod firm with his smile. "We also hope all issues with your house are okay. Your assistant informed us you were having some type of plumbing issue."

A slow lift to my eyebrow had me facing Joe, who only grinned and shook my shoulders again.

"Cami told us all about the flooding," he said, dropping his hands. "And here I was starting to think you might have forgotten about today."

The men partook in a round of laughter at his comment, but all I was thinking about were the excuses that preceded me.

And the woman that came in looking like a goddess right after.

Cami had these cute, little curls sweeping across her face when she came into the room, her bangs I was guessing as she had her hair up. The tiny twists caught on her eyelashes with the steps she made in the highest heels. Her arms full of binders, she placed one in front of each of us, filling the room with her honey smell. The scent only consumed me more when she placed one of those binders in front of me, her curvy body painted in a white dress, which hugged her hips and breasts.

"Colton's never without humor as you'll all come to see," Joe said, opening that binder Cami gave him, but I was looking at Cami, shifting her way a little. The small maneuver blocked her from escaping me, and I begged her with my eyes to look at me for just a moment.

Pushing out a heavy breath, she chose to navigate the opposite way. She went behind Joe, leaving me, and since the rest of the group had their binders, she headed for the door.

"Thanks, Cami," Joe said to her, pretty much absentmindedly as that was her job, but again, I was focused on her, waiting for her to look at me.

Please see me.

Like I willed it, I got a flicker of her gaze before she looked away and closed the door behind her. It seemed she saved me again, her excuse for me being late and all that.

Swallowing, I opened my binder, seeing something familiar. The contract to join a team, join *Miami*, and when I looked up, four grins filled my eyes.

My brother's was included. His smile had been the widest, and I wasn't surprised.

"Your..." I started, swallowing hard. "You still want to make this happen? Take a chance on me?"

Because I had to admit I was... awed. I put myself and consequently this team through media hell by the mistakes I made only several weeks ago, and here they were, offering me the keys to the world, *Miami* to play with my brother.

"We stand by our players," one of the reps said, the closest to Griffin. The man placed his large hands on the binder. "And you are one of our players. At least you will be as soon as you sign on that dotted line."

Still not believing any of this, I faced Joe.

He flashed his big teeth. "Miami's graciously offered to keep you on board with some provisions."

The rep who spoke before nodded. "A media tour being one of them," he said pointing to the contract with his hands. "You'll go from city to city, speaking on behalf of yourself and telling your own story. The details are all written out in the contract as far as what cities and the tour's length, but the purpose is to give you a voice, to share what you want to about who you are—"

"And that you're okay."

I lifted my gaze to my brother who'd said the words, his head tilted.

"That's what's most important, Colt. To Miami," Griff said, nodding. "To everyone."

He meant to him, himself and our family, and I could read between the lines. They may have not all been here, but he was, and the way the reps were letting him take the lead on this, like he had anything to do with the negotiations at all let me know *exactly* what this was. Griffin vouched for me with these people, their golden boy.

Another person to save me.

"So what do you say, Colt?" Joe pushed, putting his finger to the paper. "You want to give this all another shot? Move forward? Miami's willing to give you all the time you need, and if you do need more, that's okay."

"It's more than okay." Griffin again, Griffin taking care of me.

Panning, I did little to watch four pairs of eyes before grabbing a pen in front of me. Clicking it, I quickly signed the documents. I could give them the tour they wanted and I was okay with that.

Because *I* was okay.

Cami

"Cami?"

Colton shouldn't have been able to sneak up on me, my back turned to him in Joe's office. I'd been in deep thought trying to figure out next moves.

I'd been in deep thought trying to figure out him.

Gaining, Colton pressed his hard body up against my backside, my response apparently not quick enough for his liking. Sneaking his fingers to combine with mine, he intertwined our digits. The maneuver had been quick and too easily conducted. He'd gotten too close to me so rapidly.

What made it all worse was how much I liked it.

I liked him this close, his body warm and his fingers heaven with mine. It was like we were an actual thing or something.

A thing that shouldn't happen.

But we were, his fingers squeezing from his position behind me. He lowered what I knew to be massive height.

"Can we talk?" he asked me, his voice a whisper. It traveled so much heat along my earlobe. His swallow was audible. "Please. I need to—"

He never got to finish the statement, and in only moments, his fingers let go of mine. He backed away, and I knew why before I even turned. His brother had said his name.

I saw his brother Griffin when I did turn, the man just as massive as Colton.

"You're not getting away that easily," Griffin said to Colton. Grinning, he wrapped a long arm around his little brother's shoulders. With their expansive heights, the pair resembled gladiators, two sizable men, and I knew this was consistent in their family. Colton's brother Brody was also quite large and could probably pull a semi if met with the challenge. They also had another brother Hayden who may have lacked in build but was tall just the same. I figured this all came from their dad, a Texas man with an intimidation factor just as present as those I'd come across from my time living in New York. It was in a different way, but still there whenever I'd seen him at events with Colton. He wasn't just big, but talented too. He owned a furniture business that all his sons were heavily involved in.

Griffin brought his hands down Colton's shoulders.

"This one was a rock star in there," Griffin said about

Colton, and one could definitely tell the pair were brothers with their smooth jawlines and handsome physiques. Colton almost looked like a before picture to his older brother's after. Griffin had the polish and grace of a defined athlete, a maturity not just from his dress and the way he carried himself but his personality and overall attitude. He had some life experience under his belt and I wondered if I was staring into a detailed scope of who Colton would be one day. Griffin clearly had himself together and it showed anytime I'd come to find myself around him. It only matched what his wife put off, a woman I did aspire to be like one day. She too had herself together. They both did.

"I'm sure he was," I said to Griffin, knowing when Colton was put in professional situations he had no problem enacting his Texan charm. "And I hear congratulations is in order."

They'd given him a second chance, and Joe had let that slip before the meeting.

"Like there was any doubt," Griffin said, shaking him, and Colton's bright blue eyes veered away. Clearly his brother's fawning was putting him on the spot.

I also knew his attention was preoccupied with something else moments ago. It'd been preoccupied *on me* when his focus should have been on something else more important.

Ignoring my thoughts, I made myself smile. Griffin's arm dropped from Colton's shoulder, and when it did, Griffin squeezed Colton's arm.

"Lunch," Griffin said to him, his grin wide. "I'm buying. And, Cami?" Griffin paused, looking at me. "Join us, please. We need to celebrate what this guy did today."

For the first time during this conversation, Colton's attention pricked. His gaze in all its intensity zoomed in my direction, a hope within it that resembled what I heard in his voice only moments ago.

I also witnessed it in his text messages even before that.

I saw his messages as they came in and ignored them all. They should have never happened. *We* shouldn't have happened, and I was grateful for what happened this morning with one of his girlfriends. Sometimes a girl needed a reminder.

If anything for herself.

My smile forced, I tried not to let that show, shaking my head.

"You two should have your time," I said to them. "I'd just be in the way."

"You wouldn't."

Colton's protest came before even Griffin's could, more of that desperation easily noticeable. This went unbeknownst to Griffin. The man merely smiled before panning to me.

"He's right, Cami. You wouldn't," Griffin said. "I'd love to have you along if you want to come."

But the thing was I didn't want to come. I didn't want to drag something on or lead Colton and myself down a path that only got more and more confusing as the time went by.

Lowering, I grabbed my purse from the office's coffee table. "I think I'll pass this time, but you guys have a good time."

"Cami..." Colton's frown followed my name.

I shook my head.

"Please." I urged them to go with a push to the air. "Seriously, have a good time. I have some things to finish up here." After all, I was his assistant.

Or had he forgotten that?

I could see he had in his eyes, his brother's arm once again coming around him.

Guiding Colton away, Griffin got out a pair of keys, saying he'd drive as he had a rental car. The pair left down the hallway, intercepting my assistant, Tommy, as he came in. He'd left to get us some coffee and handed me mine.

"Things all good?" he asked me, noticing my stare in the direction where the men left.

I shrugged him off. "Of course," I lied. He really didn't want or need to know about all my drama.

I only wished I could be so lucky.

Ten

COLTON

"I COME ALL the way over here to save your little tail, and you repay me by trying to dip out on me?"

My brother Griff had his hands on the wheel, cruising his rented Range Rover amongst what had come to be my playground over the years. The streets of LA ran hot today, millennials everywhere rocking their shorts and little dresses. Living here had been a sharp contrast from the way I grew up, the epitome of lower middle class. We'd sometimes traveled into an even lower rung when my family was in the rough of it. We'd all been raised to value what we had with our hardworking father, so when I went off to college and eventually made my way here, the opulence had been more than unnerving. I'd gotten overwhelmed by it and still did on the daily, my actions reflecting that more than I liked sometimes. This place was easy to give in to.

Especially when you got everything you wanted.

Those initial years were *rough*, and though I was still trying to get a handle on it, I was making my way. It helped to have someone who traveled that road before me, my brother Griff basically forging a path not many years before me. Each step I made had only been ventured before, and I often used him as a reference.

Maybe I should stop after what he said.

"No one asked you to do that," I said to him. I suspected he helped me secure my spot with Miami, and now he confirmed it. He got me back in with those guys, put in an obvious good word for me. I shook my head. "You shouldn't have done that."

"I know I didn't have to," he said, turning to me. "But it never hurts to have a little help."

Gazing away, I faced the road, watching those locals again. We remained silent for a little while before he spoke again.

"What do you want to eat?" he asked me, always doing that grin. "I've been to LA a million times, but I'd like to see it through your eyes."

It was hard to continue being mad when he did shit like that, being all genuine or whatever. He shook my leg, and my smile couldn't be helped. I told him to take us to In-N-Out Burger.

His grin only widened.

"That's why we're brothers," he said, navigating that way.

He traveled the streets through my eyes like he said, taking the paths I told him to choose, and I guided us to my favorite chain branch. This one in particular had a great view of the ocean and a place for us to go without being pestered by the paparazzi. Being by myself, I'd get swarmed, but getting burgers with my all-star brother was basically a sure-fire bet we'd shut down the place. We called in our order ahead, and after the staff slid it to us in the back, Griffin took us to see that ocean, the sun at its highest that day.

"I'm fucking ravenous," he said, taking a big ole bite out of that chargrilled goodness. The succulent juices I had my way with as well when I unwrapped mine and the cabin of the car filled with the smell. Eventually, we put down the windows and just let the day in.

Griffin threw an arm out the window. He'd taken that stuffy suit jacket off and now just looked like my brother, his sleeves rolled up and casual. It was hard to believe we used to be those innocent country boys once upon a time, and now, we were men taking on the world. We'd both come a long way. Especially him and that wonderful family he had on the other side of the country.

"Jackson and Roxie get home all right?" I asked him, not sure if he'd actually seen them since I knew he'd been in Texas while they visited me.

The guy's face lit up at the reference of his family. "They did. She called me," he said. "And Pop says hi, as well as Ann, Hayden, Karen, and the kids—"

"Brody?" I asked. I had to say I didn't hear a lot from him besides the occasional phone call or text on his end.

I think that had to do with the twins.

The little wonders had hit their terrible twos, and he and his wife, Alexa, had their hands full. Alexa also ran a dance studio, and with Brody doing his truck driving for the family business like I knew he did, I was sure my big brother was still all over the place like he always was.

Griffin's lips lifted as he stared out into the ocean.

"Always running," he said, facing me. "I didn't see him or Alexa there, but the twins were with Gram and Aunt Robin when I stopped by. They're all doing okay. Asked about you."

Of course they did, my gaze turning away. Crumbling up my wrapper, I made a ball then tossed it out the window. The wrapper circled the rim of the trash can I'd been aiming for and when it went in, I figured I'd get some nods of acknowledgment from Griffin.

Not a damn frown.

In all honesty, the expression set me back a bit. My older

brother was always grinning. Well, he wasn't grinning now, and he was shooting the disapproving expression right at me.

"What do you want me to say, Griff?" I said, shrugging as I lounged in my seat. "I mean, tell them what they want. Tell them that I'm fine."

"And are you then?" he questioned, his expression serious. "Fine? Because you know I won't be lying to our family. Lying to Pop and Gram. Colt, if you need help—"

His aim at an intervention caused my laughter, the chuckle dry in my throat. I faced him. "I got help remember. I'm cured of my drug and alcohol addiction. The clinic said."

"I'm not talking about that," he responded with, and my attention shot to him. It unsettled me what he said, and suddenly, I wasn't happy he drove.

If he didn't, I could have peeled off.

I could have ran, dropped him off at the closest airport and been done with all this talk. Of course it wouldn't have all settled there, though. He'd come back, come for me.

They *all* would.

My family was incredibly close, and Griff and I had even stronger ties. We were like the same person, bonded as we were the youngest. He was like me so he *got* me, different in the sense that Brody and Hayden were closer to Pop. Griffin had taken care of me personally in ways the others hadn't. He looked out for me, the epitome of a big brother.

He was doing that presently, his swallow hard in his throat.

"I didn't come over here to ream you or rattle you," he said, pushing his hand behind his neck. "Whatever you're going through is obviously personal, but don't continue to hide behind the bullshit of drugs, alcohol, and an addiction when you've never shown any signs of that behavior before. It's condescending, and none of us are stupid people, Colt."

His words made it hard to breathe, made it hard to *think*,

and I really needed to get out of here. I aimed for the door, but Griffin grabbed my arm.

He wouldn't let me run away.

Squeezing me, he waited until I faced him, only then did he let go.

"Like I said, whatever's going on—if there is something going on—is all you," he said. "Just know we're not trying to get in your business. We're just concerned, and that's not even the reason why I came to LA today. Yeah, I spoke to the team about you, but I had other reasons for making my way to the city. Things outside of everything that happened with you."

Confused, I shook my head, and things only got more intense the longer he went without speaking. Griffin placed his arm out the window again, and that tension stiffened his jaw.

"I heard from Momma, Colt," he stated, what he said pinning me to my seat. "Mom. Our birth mom."

It was as if the record scratched and the scene had paused. He hadn't said what I thought he had.

He hadn't mentioned our birth mom.

His nod at my shock told me he did, an understanding between both of us. We'd been raised by a single father who had help from family—her family, our mom.

"Wait. What?" I questioned, my thoughts trying to catch up. "Our mom—"

"Momma, yeah." She was "Momma" to him, as he was old enough to remember her. I'd only been a baby when she left us. Pop said things got too hard for her and she took off. Outside of that, I'd only heard the stories from my brothers, stories about addiction in our family.

Our mother was the center.

"What did," I started, swallowing hard. "What did she say or..."

I didn't know what to say or what to question him about her.

I couldn't because I didn't know what he knew.

I sat stark still in my brother's rental car, waiting, and eventually, he pushed a hand down his face.

"I didn't actually see or interact with her," he said, breathing deep. "She just tried to reach out to me, but apparently, couldn't get *to me* so she went for Roxie. She approached her in a shopping mall. Can you believe that shit—"

"When?" I asked, and his gaze shot my way. I shook my head. "I mean, why? Why would she do that?"

His expression hardened. "Because she's selfish," he said. "She's a wrecked woman and wants to disrupt people's lives. You know she used to take us to bars as kids and lied to Pop about where she took us?"

I did know, hearing the stories. Again, I'd been too young to be aware of what was going on firsthand.

I put my hands in my lap. "What did she want?"

His shoulders lifted with his shrug. "No idea. Roxie wasn't having that bullshit. She had her security team with her. Momma explained who she was, and Roxie promptly had her escorted away. It was probably money, though. Wouldn't surprise me."

I said nothing, silent, and his hand cupped my shoulder.

"I just wanted to warn you," he said. "She came for me, so I wouldn't put it past her to come for you too. Roxie and I have dealt with stuff like this before. People coming out of the woodwork and wanting stuff. It's not foreign to us, but thankfully, our situation righted itself. It might not be so lucky with Momma, so if she does come around, I don't want you having anything to do with her. You don't know her like Brody, Hay, and I do. You were too young, and she could take advantage of you."

"I can handle myself," I told him, and he nodded.

"You're a Chandler," he said. "So I know that, but even

still, it doesn't hurt to have a warning. Hayden and Brody know what happened, but we're trying to keep this on the DL from Pop. It'll just mess him up, hurt him, and that's not necessary."

It would hurt him. My hands wrestled in my lap.

"Anyway, hopefully it won't be a problem with you being over here for a little while yet," he said. "I would have told you sooner, but you went away. Didn't want you to have to deal with that."

That was good looking out on his part, I supposed.

Griffin started the car.

"But let me know if something ever happens," he said, resting an arm on the wheel. "We didn't hear from her that long ago. Actually, right before you went away."

I nodded and he placed a hand on my head, shaking it before putting the truck into drive and pulling away. He made no more mention of the topic as we drove and I knew he wouldn't.

If anything for my sake.

Eleven

CAMI

"Tommy, I really don't have time to talk right now," I said to him, taking the last box of my stuff out to my car. I passed Irene on the way, Colton's housekeeper nodding at me. I didn't miss how she stood at the door during every pass I made by her.

Or how her eyes were somber each time.

Her hand lifted when I made it to my car that final time, waving, and she only closed the door to Colton's place after I got inside my Jetta. Her head down, she seemingly let go of the situation. She let go of me, and I guess I had to let go of everything too. I didn't know what the future held for my boss and me.

But I did know what the future held for Colton and me.

I was enacting that future as I started the car. Touching the dials, I transferred my call from my headset to my car's speakers. Tommy had called right as I'd been about to leave Colton's house for a new place to stay.

"I get it. You're busy, but you're not too busy for this," Tommy said, all of what he stated basically one breath. "It concerns Mr. Chandler and—"

I hated that he got my attention upon mentioning Colton. I hated that I *cared*, and closing my eyes, I pushed some of my curls behind my ear.

"Whatever it is about him can wait until tomorrow," I said, tossing my head back into my seat. "I've got too much on my mind right now."

And one of those things concerned finding a hotel. I'd be staying in one until my apartment got fixed, and after that, I didn't know because, honestly, going back to that place was the last thing I wanted right now. Another thing I didn't want was to go back to work tomorrow. I'd be facing repercussions for leaving Colton's house without saying a word. They wouldn't be monetary or disciplinary but consequences just the same. He'd want to talk about... things.

Not ready for that, I shifted my attention to Tommy. He was still going a mile a minute about Colton, and giving up, I crossed my arms and sat back.

"Slow down," I said. "One more time again. I'm listening now."

"Good, because it's important," he huffed. "Remember those charity vouchers I was working on? For Mr. Chandler?"

The fact that he continued to call Colton that when the man told him time and time again to use his name made me lift my eyes to the ceiling.

"Of course I remember," I said. "What about them?"

"Well, I was looking over things again tonight and um... one of them is fake."

"Fake?" I shot off the seat, my eyes widening. He definitely gotten my attention. "Fake? How so?"

"How about in every way, Cam," he told me, his voice really going a mile a minute at this point. He breathed deeply. "He's been paying out on it for about a year. It's called Project Margaret, and I can't find any evidence that it's a reputable charity of any kind. The funds even filter to a personal bank account. That's what set off red flags and allowed me to find it."

How had I missed that? I'd been the one to do the vouchers for Colton before Tommy had, and I wouldn't have missed such a thing.

You would if you'd been distracted by your boss, obsessed.

And maybe I had been a little back then. Maybe I had been the entire time while working for him and just didn't know it. I passed the feelings and intentions off as actual work when, in the back of my mind, I held a fascination with him that hadn't made itself known to me. I'd fallen into the trap most women had around him, and it was easy to do. He could be entirely too sweet sometimes and thoughtful. I mean, he even opened his house to me, and like I said, he'd always been kind. It got to me in ways that cracked the professional level, and I betrayed myself with him. I betrayed everything I stood for when coming here. I wanted a clean slate upon arrival to LA when all I ended up doing was recreating history in a new place.

It was a history that sobered me when I reached behind and grabbed my laptop from the back seat. Sitting in Colton's gated driveway, I opened it.

"Did you Google it?" I asked him, typing in my password. "Call the bank? Ask about the account?"

Because I really didn't believe it. Colton Chandler didn't have a fraudulent bone in his body, and that's what this could boil down to come tax time.

"Done and done," Tommy went on, a slow panic in his voice. He knew the reality of all this too. Calling something a charity on the books when it wasn't could lead to nothing good. "It isn't real, Cami. I looked. I left no stone unturned. Project Margaret is a fake, and Colton's put hundreds upon thousands of dollars into it. I don't know if it's a private contribution he's doing and doesn't want it advertised—"

"It has to be that, yes," I said, also finding nothing about this charity as I searched. "That's the only thing that makes sense."

"Either way, it's fraud," he used the word. Right in my ear. "I won't pay that one this month until you can look into it more. Will you ask him about it?"

I didn't know if I felt comfortable enough, but I probably should. If anything so Colton could defend himself. I didn't owe him anything, but I did believe in him and the person he was. I just couldn't help it.

Maybe I was obsessed.

Letting Tommy go, I thanked him for the knowledge, then pulled away from the curb. I'd just left when another call came in.

"Hello?" I questioned, the epitome of mind-fucked. My thoughts still consumed by Tommy's call and everything else before that I was more than frazzled. "I'm sorry. Who is this?"

The number had been unlisted when I answered.

"I'm sorry. I'm Jonathan Parker, manager and part owner of The Luxe."

"The Luxe?" I asked. "As in the bar?"

"Yes, ma'am. Exactly that. You're a Ms. Camille, right? Personal assistant to Mr. Colton Chandler? He told us as such, told us to call you."

My foot slammed the breaks at a red light. "Um, yeah, that's me. What's going on? Is Colton okay?"

"He's fine, Ms. Camille," he said, which only let me breathe a little. I mean, the man had called me because of Colton after all. Mr. Parker sighed heavily into the phone. "The problem resides in the disturbance he's caused. We had to take his keys and—"

"His keys? Why?"

"Well, because he's drunk, Ms. Camille," he stated, sobering me. "He's drunk, and as one of our more valued patrons, we felt it was important to see he was properly taken care of to get home. We offered to provide personal transportation for him, but he's adamant about not taking it. We hoped to have better luck with a personal contact. With some prompting he did allow us access to his phone, to get a number and call you. He'd only let us call you."

I closed my eyes, the light thankfully red. When some honks sounded behind me, I knew it wasn't any longer, and I peeled into traffic, typing the bar's location into the navigation system.

"I'll be right there," I told the man, thanking him for calling me. I was glad he called me and not anyone else because at this point?

I might be the only person in this city to get through to him.

~

I had the manager shut down Colton's section of the bar for privacy purposes. The Luxe was basically the paps' stomping grounds considering how many celebrities moved in and out of it, and as I'd been told Colton was in one of the VIP sections. That made closing it off easy. They restricted his area and would do so long enough for me to get him out. After that...

Well, I didn't know. I had no idea what was going on with someone I thought I was really starting to know. I had worked with Colton closely and even closer in the past few months. He trusted me, and I had been starting to trust him, but each and every passing day and hour seemed to give me a reason not to. He was a man of his own thoughts, actions, and keeping them close to the vest, he didn't allow me to be privy to any of it. He didn't allow anyone to be, his secrets only with him. I didn't know who he was turning into or if he'd always been that person, and when the manager pushed the double doors open, I got to see another side. I saw Colton hunched, slumped over a tumbler glass while he sat in a privacy booth. I saw Colton at a heavy low, and when he lifted that glass to take another drink, he saw me.

Eyes of a normally bright blue panned over to me, slow and dull like the light had been ripped clear out of them. They were also red-rimmed, a darkness underneath I hadn't seen in even his most rigorous days of training. I'd seen Colton tired. I had seen Colton exhausted.

I'd never seen Colton defeated.

He seemed that way upon taking his drink, the swallow hard as the liquid traveled down his throat. His gaze appraising me, he caused my approach to pause full stop.

His eyes narrowed. "You've come to talk to me *now*," he said, shaking his glass before taking another drink. He forced it down harder than he had before, his jaw ticking after he did. "Why is it I only get your attention when I'm like this?"

The words seemed to be spoken more to himself than to me, but that didn't make them cut any less. Placing my bag down, I sat beside him.

His gaze followed every move.

Pausing, I simply sat there with him at first, not wanting to upset him by saying the wrong thing. He was clearly upset. I just didn't understand why.

"I've come to take you home," I said to him, braving myself up. Other than the incident at his house, I'd never seen him this way. I mean, he'd been drunk before but only in good fun and nothing ever like this. He also never got publicly intoxicated. If he let loose, it was usually at one of his own parties or amongst friends. Today was neither of those situations.

Colton's gaze veered again, moving to the manager and his staff. They all stayed at the door, close enough for Colton to see from his booth. He sat back. "You've come to help them throw me out," he settled on, tossing his head back. He closed his eyes. "I didn't do anything wrong. It was that girl. I didn't want her. I..."

His eyes falling open, he started to explain the incident, which caused the staff to cut him off—an incident that had been explained to me when I arrived. With his celebrity status, Colton easily gained attention the moment he set foot in this place. The thing was, he wanted time alone I guess, and when other patrons followed him to his booth, a woman in particular...

It escalated rather quickly. He raised his voice at her, a voice I'd personally never heard at an octave above calm. He had the epitome of patience, this man. Especially when he'd been with me.

Crossing my arms over my lap, I leaned his way.

"This isn't like you," I said to him, making his eyes close again. "You don't do things like this. Did something happen at lunch? With your brother?"

He'd been fine before. I mean, he hadn't been particularly happy—I turned him down for lunch with Griffin, but I believed he would get over it quickly. Anxiety surged that maybe this outburst had to do with me, but that couldn't be possible.

I didn't miss Colton's smirk on his lips. He took another drink, then shook his head after it.

"Nothing happened with my brother," he said to me, his light eyebrows descending. "And how would you know what I'm like?"

"I felt I was starting to," I told him, patient but also not willing to put up with the attitude that seemed to surface my way. I didn't deserve it. My jaw stiffened. "I mean, we've worked together for years, Colton."

"Mmhmm, yes. A while now," he stated, a clear sarcasm in

his voice. He shook his glass. "And you'd think I'd get some allowances for that. You talking to me if you had an issue with me. You *listening* when there's a misunderstanding." His throat jumped. "You'd think I would get something."

He was obviously referencing what happened earlier in the day, but nothing I saw personally could be misunderstood about finding a woman in his bed only hours after he'd gone down on me. All that rang pretty freaking clear.

And had nothing to do with this situation now.

I stood. "We need to go now, Colton. The people who run this place like you, but if you ever want to set foot here again—"

"The people here like my money," he challenged, facing me. "And I don't give a shit what they think."

My head shot back. "I don't know what the hell your problem is, but I have to say, I don't like this side of you I'm seeing. You don't do this crap. Getting drunk, getting... wasted in a public place. This *isn't* like you. Now, I don't get what's going on, but you better get it together. Going out like this and causing a spectacle is unacceptable. I represent you and who you are, and I can't keep doing that if you keep putting me in positions like this. I thought I knew you, Colton. But between stuff like this and the charity vouchers thing..."

His gaze shot to me in an instant, and I closed my eyes. I slipped up saying something, and he noticed.

His eyes narrowed. "What about charity vouchers?"

I supposed I couldn't avoid this. He asked me a question.

I opened my hands. "Tommy stumbled across something while he was paying your charity contributions."

"What kind of something?"

"He questioned the legitimacy of one of them," I said, frowning at him. "And looking into it, I do too, a Project Margret? Whatever it is doesn't lead to an actual nonprofit.

The funds go to a clear private bank account, and the thing is, we're wondering why."

We needed answers from him, and staring at him, I got lost in those dull blue eyes.

"You've assumed something about me," he stated taking another drink. This one made him wince. "And it sounds like you've already made up your mind."

"But I haven't," I told him, being honest about that. I wanted to hear the truth. I wanted him to tell me, *talk* to me. "What is it, Colton? Why have you—"

"Done nothing wrong," he said looking at me. "I'm just as guilt-free in this as I am anything else when it comes to you."

"Colton—"

"It's a private venture," he said, nodding his head. "And you won't find anything wrong there because there's nothing to find. Jesus, Cami. It's a private endeavor, and it will remain private because I prefer it that way. Project Margret is personal, and as it's my money, I don't have to answer to either you or Tommy, or any of your accusations."

I cringed at his cut and how cold he'd been when he said it. Things didn't have to be that way at all, but he'd taken them to that place.

He pushed his hands over his shaven head.

"Just know it's legit," he said to me, turning his head. "And it's classified the way it is because it's personal."

"Why wouldn't you just tell me that?" I said. "Why leave me to find it? To think God knew what about you—"

"Would it have mattered?" he asked me, making me draw back. His blond eyebrows descended. "You'd listen to that like you did this morning? About Skylar? I know she's why you left."

The breaths left my lips in a slow current.

I pushed my hair behind my ear. "You and Skylar are none of my business."

"That's the thing, Cami. There is no me and Skylar. There's Skylar and then there's me and her being at my house this morning was completely innocent. Regardless of what you might think."

Well, that was definitely a riot. He was making me out to be more of a fool than I already was, coming down here and trying to save him from any media backlash that might come. I was trying to save *his* career.

I stood. "You forget the time I've put in with you, Colton Chandler. It's time in which I've been able to pick up on you and the type of person you are."

"And who's that?" he asked, standing too. "Tell me, Cami. Who exactly do you think I am?"

"Someone I thought was honest!" I raised my hands. "Someone I thought was kind and sweet and didn't walk around the earth like he ran it or treat me like a fool just because I work for him. That girl was in your bed, Colton. I found her there, stark naked with your sheets pressed against her boobs, and if you're telling me that you weren't with her, that you didn't go down on her just as you had me only hours ago, then you must take me for a complete and utter idiot or maybe naive. Neither of which I am, by the way, or you wouldn't have hired me. I'm not a dense woman, Colton, so don't take me for one."

I said more than I should have, and by the time I finished, I was shaking so hard I didn't even have the thought to backpedal. I was just so angry, angry at him.

But more angry at myself.

I hated that he made me so emotional, that he'd driven me so crazy when he should be nothing more to me than my boss. He was nothing more than my boss and spinning, I might have made it out of his booth.

Had he not grabbed my arm.

He used it to advance me just as smoothly as he had the

night before, and his hard chest against my back, he was just as breathy as I was.

He leaned in.

"You're one of the smartest, most intelligent women I've ever known, Camille," he said breathing those words down my ear, my neck. "And you're right, I do know that, which is why I can't get you out of my head, which is why I had to taste you. Not only do I want to do it again, the simple thought of it makes me want to blow my load right here."

The words brought surges to my body and entirely too much heat. Especially when he wrapped his arms around me and tugged me tight against his chest.

"Eating you out, pleasing you..." The groan pulsed deep from his chest. "It gave me just as much pleasure as it gave you. You're stuck in my head and unable to leave, even if I wanted that to be the case. I want you, Cami."

He wanted me.

"And not to make you come or get you a one-off." He pulled me around, forcing me to confront him full on. "But because you want this and because you want me to give it to you. I know what I said about last night being a onetime thing and know that would make things way easier than I'm making them right now."

"Colton—"

"I had no idea Skylar was in my room this morning," he admitted, his words tight. "And if I had, I would have made her leave. The only one who should have been in my bed this morning is you. I wanted it to be you."

I was shaking by the time he touched my cheek, so much honesty in his words, how he really felt about what he said. But the thing was, he didn't know what he was asking for.

Neither people did before it was too late.

I couldn't have a repeat of that, do that to myself again,

but I especially couldn't put Colton through the trials and tribulations of a professional relationship turned more.

I couldn't because I cared about him.

His fingers brushed over my cheek, and when they slid, I knew I was crying.

"Cami..."

"I can't, Colton," I said shaking my head. "I can't. We can't. I work for you."

"Then don't work for me. We can make this work—"

"I won't get in a relationship with my boss!"

The words made any pursuit he'd been about to make stop, and unable to look at him, I faced away.

"I'll call Tommy to get you," I said to him, then chose to walk away from all this, him.

I felt I had to.

Twelve

COLTON

"I can't get in a relationship with my boss."

She hadn't said she wouldn't get in a relationship with me, but she—couldn't, as if she was physically unable, and as we traveled along the tarmac toward the start of the first leg of my media tour, I watched her. Sitting with Tommy on the opposite side of our moving limo, Cami had been wrapped up with her assistant all morning. At least, pretending to be. She showed up to my house with him in tow this morning.

Because she moved out of my house.

I discovered that quickly after an Uber got me home that night at the bar. I refused to call Tommy despite Cami advising it. I wasn't incapable of taking care of myself, regardless of what she may think.

Why did she say she can't?

I figured that had ninety percent to do with me and less with her. I hadn't been portraying my best self lately when it came to her. Hell, I hadn't been to myself either. It was drastically clear people in my life were noticing the positions I continued to place myself in, one of impulse and carelessness.

My brother had been more than obvious when he came down to see me, then later that night with Cami...

I refused to believe her denial was all me. I mean, I'd done some fucked-up crap recently, but I owned it, and I had a feeling she was doing the opposite. She avoided my gaze since the bar, avoided me. I couldn't even get a word in with her today, her assistant, Tommy, a body between us. He kept her talking, engaging with her on other things having to do with business and the tour.

I caught her gaze around Tommy's head, and before I could get any words to her, I lost her sight. Cami's head dipped, and her attention veered again, going over schedules and timelines. She was basically in charge of this tour I was about to go on, in charge of me, which only further let me know my power in position to hers. She had all of it.

Just like she had in other ways.

All of this was crystal clear to me as we pulled up to our private charter, the jet beautiful and shining. The staff came down the stairs to greet us, and Cami and Tommy got out before my security could open their doors for them. They didn't wait for me, and once again, Cami avoided any type of interaction. She pushed sunglasses over her eyes, and taking her direction, I did the same. I had my aviators over my face when Jerry, my head of security, stood by the door for me. After I got out, he closed the door behind me, and I scaled the stairs behind Cami and Tommy. I had to stop for a few autographs by the staff. I got that unusually a lot despite the fact that I was sure they had all kinds of celebrities bigger than me on these things. It held me up, but I was always happy to deliver. Jerry had my bag, and I went ahead and took it from him on my way inside. I had enough fawning over me today.

I dragged the thing down the aisle and immediately spotted Cami.

She was putting her own bag in the overhead compartment, her pert little navel exposed below her top. On her tiptoes, she attempted to jam in her bag, and I abandoned mine to help her.

"Let me," I said. It was easy, of course. It was just a little bag.

Cami straightened her shirt at my awareness of her, covering that cute, little belly button above her miniskirt.

"Thank you," she said, averting her gaze as she removed some of those big curls from her eyes. I loved when she wore them wild and free like that. They filled the air with a sweet smell, and I could nearly taste her. Maybe she saw that in my eyes because, as soon as I was done with her bag, she left me. Sliding past, she plopped down next to Tommy in the jet's plush leather seats. This didn't surprise me, considering her avoidance.

That didn't mean I'd make it easy for her.

I got my bag up above, then proceeded to sit across from her and Tommy. This made both their eyes widen. I normally never sat with them, but not really by choice. They usually left me my space and did their own thing. Cami chewed on the side of her lip the moment I took up occupancy, and looking at her, I spoke to Tommy.

"How about you get us some Cokes," I requested of him. "For the flight? We'll need something to drink. Cami, that's your favorite, right?"

Her eyes widened more.

"It's not yours," she said, adjusting in her seat. "Why don't you order something you like?"

"But it's what you like," I told her, sitting back. I faced Tommy again. "Tommy, Cokes, please. I'm sure the flight attendants would be happy to assist you."

This would get him away for a second, and I *needed* a second. I wasn't sure when I'd have another so I was taking this chance.

Tommy's eyes were basically playing a game of ping pong between Cami and me. Despite more than looking confused, he did get up in the end. He left Cami and me alone, and immediately, I took his seat.

"Hey," I said to her, my voice quiet. It was almost like I didn't want to scare her. I kept... scaring her, and I hated it. I hated what I seemed to be doing to her. What was worse was, each one of her drawbacks ripped away at my heart, and I wished I could fix this.

I have to fix this.

A wince hit her face, like the actual sound of my voice rattled her.

"Hi," she said, choosing to look at me. She had this restless curl that kissed her cheek, and I fought so fucking hard not to touch it.

"You moved out," I told her, getting into it right away. She'd been gone over a week, but I'd never gotten to talk to her about it. "You didn't have to, you know."

Despite what happened, she didn't. She could have stayed as long as she wanted.

Her body sighed when she pushed her head back into the seat.

"You know I did, Colton." Her jaw worked. "I never should have been there in the first place."

Maybe she shouldn't have, but it did happen, and moving closer, I wanted to remind her why she should have stayed. Why she never should have left, but my opportunity passed the moment a second car came up on the tarmac.

Panning, Cami could see the new arrivals from her seat, and at the appearance of my best friend Jesse and the woman he escorted, I knew the time for talk was over.

Madison... the *other* woman I'd been seeing outside of Skylar, made her appearance. She looked the epitome of the typical woman I usually found myself around too. She was all legs, breasts, and Victoria's Secret-length extensions. Her cloak of jet-black hair ran down her back, her curves tight and more than welcomed by Jesse, who helped her with her bags. They'd both be coming along with us today. Jesse was coming because he had some of the same promotional appearances scheduled alongside mine, but Madison had other reasons.

"She only wanted a ride," I said to Cami, knowing I'd already lost her attention when she reached down and grabbed her MacBook from under her seat. Opening it up, she ignored me. I swallowed. "She has family in New York, our first stop."

But I should have said no when she asked, and I knew the moment my explanation couldn't be heard over Camille's suddenly typing fingers. She had her campaign up, my sister-in-law Roxie's project. She got several keystrokes in before she turned with a frown.

"Then you better go to her," she said to me, and I slid my hand under those fingers before she could type again.

I looped our fingers.

"I broke up with them, Cami," I said, her touch warm as I shook my head. "Both of them, and Madison knows what this is today. It's just a ride."

"A ride that doesn't bother me." She pulled her hand away. "Because why would it bother your assistant?"

I knew it did just as clearly as her eyes left mine. Her attention traveled to Tommy who had our Cokes. He tried to hand me one as my friend and Madison got on the plane behind him.

"It's for her," I said to him, getting up. "Please, have at it." I mean, what else could I have said?

She made her position clear.

∾

Cami

Focusing on work and the keystrokes on my laptop was easier. It was *simpler* to place all my energy there instead of the one place it shouldn't have been, Colton and everything that had to do with him. Currently, those things consisted of his social activities, Jesse and... Madison. Colton's friend sat to his right and his former girlfriend to his left—and I used that title loosely. She sat quite close to Colton, using absolutely any excuse to touch him or tilt her head back at a joke he said, which really wasn't all that funny. I knew because I heard.

I heard when I was supposed to be working.

He may have broken things off, but they clearly remained friendly. Even Jesse teased him about it sometimes, shaking Colton's head. After that, Jesse threw his hands back behind his head and slept the majority of the flight to NYC. That action left Colton and Madison to themselves. They chatted together then, and most of the conversation, Colton remained silent, listening while Madison went on about whatever she did. She was quite beautiful and essentially perfect for him and the world he found himself in. She fit right in, and as the flight started to descend, he took her hand, guiding her to bend her head of lengthy dark hair. He spoke to her in her ear, and whatever he said made her smile. I unfastened my attention just as he brought her in for a hug because I had to. What they were saying was none of my business.

I made sure of that.

I couldn't provide any answers to Colton during the flight. I couldn't tell him *why* this couldn't work because I didn't have anything for him. I couldn't get into a relationship with him because that was my choice. The decision was something he also should take stake in, as he should be focusing on himself and the purpose of these next few days. This trip was about him and his career, and it definitely wasn't about *me*. We grounded, and the man of the hour got up from his seat. His friends joined him, and while they did, I figured it was important to start getting down to business as to what this trip was about.

"We should probably go over your first feature in the car," I tossed to Colton, gaining his attention. He and his friends had all been trying to get their bags from above, and I reached up and got mine too. "Just so you're prepared," I stated. "We never got to do that during the flight."

I didn't dare go over to him while he was in the middle of a conversation with his former girlfriend—again, I used that term loosely. They were close now, even standing.

And he had his arm around her.

I mean, he had his arm around Jesse too, I supposed, slapping his friend's back before allowing him to stride down the aisle. In response to what I said, Colton simply said one word, "Cool," before tipping his chin and placing his hand to the small of Madison's back. She grabbed him too, leaning her head in and laughing at another joke he said or something.

The sigh shouldn't have been in my breath, but it was as I got my stuff together. I got my rolling bag to the ground.

"You need help, Cam?" Tommy asked me, and I shook my head. I didn't need help.

At least not in this way.

Once inside the tiny airport, Colton's party sectioned off. Jesse got in line to get airport coffee while Colton and Madison lingered closer in my vicinity. I could see them well as they snuck off to their little corner. They hugged again, and when Colton went to pull away, Madison didn't. There was a hesitation in her arms, like she didn't want to let go.

Squeezing her, Colton gave into the embrace, tiling his head to whisper something to her. He seemed as if he actually was ending it. Especially when he pulled back and framed her face. He spoke right to her, straight on so there was no confusion, before pulling her back in to give her one final hug. Breaking away, he lifted his hand to wave. He waved to her while she pulled her own bag toward the exit doors, and I didn't understand all this.

In fact, it actually made me angry.

I didn't want him to break things off. *Especially* for my benefit if that's what he was doing. He only made things more complicated when they shouldn't have been. We wouldn't make whatever *thing* that had happened between us work, and I stood by that.

That was until I saw him.

Coming down the escalator, a man of a familiar height and build took my attention, handsome and cut in all the ways a man should be and easily distracting. He distracted *me* with his sultry hazel eyes and deep, black hair styled in the fashion of a business man. In a fine suit, he wore the business side of him well and actually was one of the top marketing execs in his field. I knew because he was my mentor directly out of college.

I knew because I *dated* him.

Stepping back, my heart raced in the fashion of a baby bird, rapid and intense. Especially, when those steps I made to flee did the exact opposite of what they'd been supposed to do. I caught Taylor's attention the moment I moved, and when he raised his hand...

"Cami?" he called, starting to head my way, and seeing Colton, I grabbed him.

Colton hung back. "What—"

"Pretend you're with me," I rushed, my eyes only on Taylor. He was moving right toward us, right toward me.

Colton eyed me. "What are you talking about?"

"I said just pretend you're with me. Pretend we're together, *please*. I need you to."

Colton couldn't have looked more confused, and considering Taylor was almost here, he didn't have the time to stand around and figure it out.

I squeezed his arm. "Do you get it? Understand what I said?"

"I do, but you said..."

I knew what I said. I did, but that was moments ago. It was moments before *now* and Taylor, my ex, was right upon us. He came closer with his dashing smile and smoldering good looks that had taken me easily back then. I'd been naive and, like I said, fresh out of college. If I hadn't been, I might have seen him for who he was.

Someone who could potentially ruin my life.

Taylor arrived with a widened grin. "Cami?"

"Hi, Taylor," I stated, the brick wall beside me still firm. Colton wasn't making any moves, and I worried he wouldn't. He'd just leave me standing there, frozen like a deer in headlights in front of the guy I used to date. The bastard actually had the nerve to reach over to me once he got to us.

He reached over to give me a hug.

The nausea consumed me as I was forced to give in to it out of politeness, arms around me that never did feel quite right. I should have known that then. I should have *known*. Even from the beginning, Taylor had never been all that giving with himself, and that went from something as simple as his time to other far more intimate things. He kept me tied in a relationship that was literally going nowhere, but I'd been too starstruck by who he was and that he'd chosen me as his protégé. He plucked me right out of college to work at his business firm, and in that time, he led me to believe he actually cared about me.

That he even loved me.

But there had never been love, and my awareness of that resurfaced the moment his arms went around me for that "friendly" embrace. It was affection I wanted to flee from and, eventually, was gratefully saved from it.

Colton's hand, his warm and inviting touch, came to rest

gently on my back. He stood there, close and almost as if he acted as a reminder. His touch told me he was there and would remain until I came back, until I came home. There he was when I got out of the hug, standing above me with his hand in his pocket. Guiding me back, he let me come to him.

He pushed a hand over my shoulder. "Cami, who's your friend?"

Who. Was. My. Friend? Such a simple question, but then again, it wasn't. Yes, I knew this man, hugged him, but he wasn't my friend. In fact, he was the exact opposite.

Because he was the reason I ultimately had to leave New York City.

I left hurt, defeated, and this man had been the reason why, this man and his arrogance. He couldn't accept that I didn't want to be with him, that there was no spark between us, regardless of what he'd done for me. He'd been selfish, and for a man of his caliber, it hadn't been surprising. Taylor Reed was a businessman, successful, and once upon a time, he had been my mentor. This man taught me everything I needed to know outside of business school, and his tutelage had been the reason I easily found work when I chose to come to LA in the end. I truly valued him for that, and he was a gifted teacher.

But that didn't mean he owned me, and some of me truly thought he still believed he did. His audacity to reach in and give me a hug after all that happened between us... told me that.

I moved in closer to Colton. "This is Taylor," I said, not breaking my eye contact with my ex. "We used to see each other."

That was putting it mildly. He ruled my life for almost an entire year because I'd been too young and naive to notice he'd been actually doing it. I believed I loved him once upon a time, which was foolish. Love wasn't having to completely abide by someone else's schedule or turning a blind eye to whenever that person chose to look at another woman—which he frequently did. He walked all over me, and I honestly had been too scared to leave. When I ultimately had to leave New York because of him, he showed me I had a reason to be.

"We did," he chose to say, clearly analyzing the situation as his honeyed irises shifted between Colton and me. He obviously noticed—us and, I wagered, was trying to figure out what to do with the situation presented before him. "For about a year," he said, finally finding my eyes. He smiled a little. "Seems like a lifetime ago, though."

The audacity of the statement had me wanting to share a few words, which I ultimately chose to keep in. What seemed like a lifetime for him was every day for me, every time I looked out my window and saw a new environment, not because I wanted to but had to. I could never work in New York City again thanks to my relationship with him, and I was reminded of that every day.

Pocketing his hands, Taylor tipped his chin at Colton. "Who's your friend, Cami? Or are you going to leave me to wonder?"

I'd prefer not to introduce my new boss to my old one, but since we were here, I had to do something. "This is Colton, my, um..."

"Boyfriend," Colton just went ahead and finished for me. He obviously was playing into all I'd set up, and I was grateful. Especially when he made his arm snug around me. There was so much comfort in the action I dared not admit and probably wouldn't when it was over.

For obvious reasons.

This entire situation was messed up, but thankfully for me, my new boss was putting up with it. He stapled on that heartbreaker smile, bringing a hand down my arm.

"You're both headed to the city, then?" Taylor asked us.

He straightened his bag over his arm. "May I ask, business or pleasure?"

"I'd have to say both," Colton chimed in, smiling a little. "I'm traveling for work and didn't want to make her wait for me. Be bored at home? You know how that is."

Taylor's brown eyes panned to me. "I'm sure you wouldn't be bored with this one at all," he said tilting his head. "Definitely gave me a run for my money while we were together."

Meaning, I challenged him, which he definitely hadn't liked. Men like Taylor, powerful in their industries, were used to getting everything they wanted. They were used to followers while they were leaders. He led me down a path I readily took, until I'd become smart enough to know I didn't deserve it. I deserved both his time and affection, his love, and when I didn't get either of those, I chose to walk.

He didn't like that.

He didn't like it enough to ruin my life. He made it so I could never work in New York City again with his influence. It was the ultimate reason I ended up in LA and working for Colton in the first place. Each prospective job I had in NYC after leaving Taylor's firm led to canceled interviews, and any offers I had prior were shut down before I could even sign the paperwork. He essentially blackballed me from acquiring any work in *his* city.

And he did it without a sweat.

The hurt, the pain, instantly resurfaced at those thoughts, and I moved closer to Colton. Like he knew what I needed, he came closer too. His hold on me warm, he clasped my arm securely. He didn't let me go, staring down at me.

"Well, she's very special," Colton responded with, my heart squeezing in response. He rubbed my arm. "I'm only sorry another guy had to lose out for me to have that."

It had been absolutely the perfect thing for him to say and

sounded so genuine I thought he actually meant what he said. As if they weren't just words or an act for him. They sounded real, and I had to shut that possibility out of my mind.

Otherwise, I'd be the one to ruin the act in the end.

"I hope you have a safe trip wherever you're going," Colton said to Taylor, smiling, and I bet, knowing him, he did mean that, what he just said. "If you're going by chartered jet too, it's nice, good snacks."

Taylor only looked at him. I was sure he didn't know what to do. He'd looked even more out of sorts than I had initially.

I held Colton tighter, enjoying his warmth when I had no right to. It wasn't meant for me. I made sure of that, hadn't I? I'd chosen a different route, and I did so because of this man before us, my old boss, Taylor. He was a guy I still couldn't get out of my head, even after all this time. I would have liked to think he never owned me, that he never held a claim on me, but some of that would always remain a little untrue. Some of what he'd done still affected me, a tiny bit of that hurt still there, and I guess it traveled with me all the way to LA.

"Enjoy your time in the city," Taylor chose to say, and really, what else could he have said? Colton had the win here, and like Colton had said, he got to have it because Taylor missed out.

Lifting his hand, Taylor waved his goodbye, and almost at the same time, Colton let go of me.

"Thank you," I said to him, trying to find his eyes. "I appreciate it. That guy's a real..."

"No problem." Colton had spoken the words the same time he raised his hand to Jesse, gaining his friend's attention. Bouncing, Jesse had two sets of coffee, heading over to us. Colton had started to walk that way, but I braced his arm.

"Colton, I—"

"It was really nothing, Camille," he said, his bag in hand. "But I guess it is nice to know I'm not the only one."

I frowned. "Not the only one in regards to what?"

"To having baggage," he stated, straightforward, and then his friend arrived with his coffee.

"What did I miss?" Jesse asked, exchanging glances between us. He obviously picked up on something. He crossed his arms. "Something going on or...?"

By then, Tommy, who had *my* coffee, had also joined us. I supposed we had a big old party in the middle of the airport now.

Colton brought his coffee to his chest. "Absolutely nothing," he said, his expression grim as he stared at me. "At least not anymore."

He left me frazzled, basically dumbstruck, in front of both his friend and my assistant, but I shouldn't have been.

Because he was absolutely right.

Colton left after that, and with a shrug, Jesse went off after him.

Tommy handed me my coffee. "Everything okay, Cam?" he asked me, looking back at Colton. "I would have come over with these sooner, but..."

He'd seen something, and he didn't need to tell me to let me know. What was basically an atom bomb explosion occurred right here only moments ago, and if he'd been paying even a shred of attention, he'd know something was up between Colton and me.

Passing it off, I blew on my coffee.

"Everything used to be," I told Tommy, being honest. "That was... until me."

Thirteen

CAMI

THE EVENTS that occurred in New York basically set the tone for the rest of the trip. Colton partook in his various promotional activities and pretty much ignored me the rest of the time when he didn't have to listen to me. I kept his schedule, made sure he got to where he needed to be, and he basically treated the situation as such. I worked for him.

And he made that clear.

His stop at ESPN, where we went to in New York, proved to be more than fruitful. He showed up with a smile, cracking a few jokes in his muscle tee, and when things got serious in the conversation, he did too. He talked about his situation pertaining to drugs and alcohol—by the grace of God, the media hadn't picked up on the events at The Luxe not that long ago—and when the topic went that way, he spoke both eloquently and as truthfully as my words allowed him to. I wrote what I was expected to write, the story about a man and the tough times he'd fallen into, but in the end, how he managed to get out. It didn't matter if that story was skewed or fabricated a little.

After all, what did the truth matter anyway?

The spectacle continued on to Indianapolis and various stops in the Midwest until we went south.

"I'd like to just get in and get out, please," he'd said during a flight to Texas. His media feature that day just happened to be an hour-and-a-half drive from El Paso.

Where his family stayed.

Whenever we were close to where his family lived, time was always put in for him to travel there. For the most part, he usually took advantage of that, but that had been well before the events that happened in LA. It'd been *before* all that drama and *my* drama with him, and I supposed if it were my family, I'd have the same position on visiting them too. Whatever the case, deciding on how to both spend and allocate his time was Colton's choice, and I ignored the phone calls that came in after we were back in the air and flying over Texas. Some of them did come to *my* phone when they couldn't get his, his family.

But everything was okay, right?

I supposed I had to believe that, forcing myself in my own world and placing my attention where it needed to be right now. The deadline with Roxie didn't stop just because I was working, and any moment I wasn't with Colton, I worked on it. I woke up early, went to bed late, and even designed during various parts of the day when Colton was doing, say, a university or park appearance. I didn't stop and I couldn't. Working on this, *Roxie's project*, was a possible means out of the situation I was currently in, and even though I always knew that was the end game, this path seemed to be a necessity now.

Especially when I crossed paths with ultra-blue eyes. I didn't catch them staring at me a lot, but when I did, it was always hard. Like during our flights when he believed I was on my laptop and not paying attention, or even worse, in long car trips when we were *all* trying to catch a few winks of sleep before Colton's next feature. I noticed sometimes he wouldn't be sleeping. Those eyes would shift and suddenly be on me, always in the distance like he'd never left.

We'd returned to California about a month into Colton's tour, but not to LA. We were more upstate, in San Francisco where Colton had a television appearance on a local talk show. He'd finished that interview quickly, moving on after answering their questions, and now was in the middle of a photo shoot with his buddy Jesse. Jesse hadn't been with us after Colton's trip to New York, doing his own schedule, but he rejoined us for Colton's activities today. Bumping fists, the guys had too much fun on set.

I supposed that had to do with the women.

Earlier that day, some of the guys' cheerleaders had joined us for a promotional shoot. They met up with us all for lunch before cruising over to the studio and posing for pictures with two of the hottest guys on the LA court. Sporting their little outfits, the ladies seemed very comfortable with both Colton and Jesse. They had to be, since they were hanging off them.

Each guy had a girl literally hanging on their biceps like zoo animals. The photographer told the players to lift the women off the floor, which they easily did. With Jesse's height, he had the girls clear off the set, but Colton did one better.

"Wrap your legs around me," he told them both, grabbing their asses to hold them up. They giggled, and spandex stretched tight over their supple asses as they got into a good position for the pictures.

The photographer chuckled. "That's great, Colton. Do you mind if the ladies give you a little kiss on the cheek?"

And what guy would, right?

Certainly not Colton, and preparing, he cheesed for the camera while the girls placed a kiss on his cheeks. He made the ladies laugh a little as he bounced them. The giggles of glee definitely made the picture look more genuine as they were in mid-smile, but the whole thing was a bit obnoxious, and I think even Jesse noticed that.

Frowning, the man actually shook his head at Colton, glancing away before taking his attention back to his own ladies. He busted out a smile as he still had a hold on his girls, but when the photographer took the photo, saying his smile was forced was an understatement. The shutter flashed, and he released the girls off his sides. Colton, on the other hand, kept his close.

Bouncing, the dancers begged him to sign their chests, which you'd think they would have enough of, considering they saw him all the time during his games. I supposed the attention never got old, though, and he gave in to them, asking for a pen. Someone handed one to him, and he moved permanent ink over their tanned, double Ds. Finding my eyes, he noticed me watching as he went for the second set, and I veered my attention.

At the shift, I found Tommy who'd also been watching the whole spectacle like I had. I used to be taken aback whenever he'd catch moments of whatever… thing Colton and I had been putting ourselves through, but over the constant days of travel, it'd been nice to have somewhat of a confidant in all this. Even if he was my assistant. He didn't know what was going on, too polite to ask I could imagine, but the man wasn't stupid. I was sure he picked up something, and it was nice to know I wasn't alone in all this drama.

Forcing a smile at him, I put out my hand. He'd thankfully brought me coffee.

"Thank you," I told him, and nodding, his attention shifted to the shoot again. Jesse had joined the group of Colton and the four ladies, and smiling, he seemed to be getting into whatever they were discussing. I bet, knowing my boss, they were setting their aims on doing some clubbing later tonight. I heard whispers of such during lunch when we sat down with the girls. I had other plans.

Not that Tommy and I were invited anyway.

"I'm going to take off," I said to my assistant. I lifted my coffee to the set. "You got this? Please tell me you got this."

I'd scheduled time ahead for my other venture. Roxie wanted the final drafts of the rebranding concepts done tonight. Knowing that, I planned to overnight copies to her I'd be picking up at the printers. I knew I didn't have to provide her physical copies, but I wanted to impress by having something in full color and physical for her to place her eyes on. I supposed that was the marketer in me, and in any sense, making the concepts in this way wasn't a problem. A local printer I looked into merely needed my final concepts. I planned to email them and they'd be printed before I even arrived. I'd ship them after that and they'd be good to go to Roxie.

I worried when this moment came—the time for me to leave—Tommy might lose a bit of his nerve. He had before when I placed him in similar situations involving Colton, but my assistant had shown me a lot through this media tour. He was tackling tasks alongside me, and I trusted him to be able to handle the rest of Colton's day.

He handed me my bag. "I'm good. Go and good luck. You deserve whatever comes from this."

Tommy's gaze panned over to Colton and party again. His frown was definitely present before he wiped it away and gave me a smile. "Hurry up. You don't want to miss your deadline."

Finding that sweet, I squeezed his arm. He was rooting for me as much as I was.

He wanted me to move on from this too.

~

Colton

I was in the middle of a text when I noticed Cami was gone, my constant awareness of her stronger than I liked most days. She'd made herself pretty damn clear where she stood in regards to us. Especially with that incident concerning her ex-boyfriend. Frankly, the whole thing more than pissed me off, and thinking back, I did act rashly when it came to the incident. I knew that moments after it occurred and took the feeling along with me on each leg of my media tour. I supposed maybe pride got in the way of actually talking to her about anything, and though I had no intentions of doing so at the present, I never did like when I couldn't find her.

I just got too used to her being there.

One could do with that what they wished, but I forced myself to put my phone away as I looked for her. I passed Jesse along the way, and thank fucking God I had my friend on board for today. I needed someone to release the tension with, and my buddy Jesse was definitely good for that. He was talking to the girls we'd been shooting with before, and I pounded his fist as I slipped by to seek out Cami.

He faced me. "Hey, Colt—"

"One sec, K? I need to find Cami."

His head tipped back with the words, his smile not quite reaching his eyes at his acknowledgement. He went back to talking with the girls, but I noticed his gaze followed me away a little before he did. I loved having him here, but he had seemed a bit moody today. He hadn't been his normally boisterous self, and I could only blame that on me, my attention divided. Between all this shit with Cami and the rest of the mess my life turned into due to previous acts, I was completely *on*, and that had everything to do with me. I was still dealing with my family, avoiding them, and after what my brother said about my mom, that lifted a whole new level of stress. Not a single member of my family had ever mentioned Momma since we were kids, and that'd only been because I pressed. I pushed them about it naturally. They remembered her, and I hadn't, so obviously, I had questions.

I shut them down when they stopped answering them.

My phone burning in my pocket, I ignored the sensation and ventured over to Tommy. Finding him was better than nothing. Technically Cami's assistant, he could tell me where she was.

"Hey, Tommy, you seen Cami?" I asked, looking around. She hadn't been on set for a long time.

Tommy lifted his head from the digital planner Camille normally had on her.

"Uh, she scheduled time off for today," he said, obviously distracted when he went back to the tablet. "Wanted to finish her project for your sister-in-law."

I closed my eyes at that, how she'd been working *even harder* since the incident that occurred in New York, and with the whispered exchanges I heard between Tommy and herself, it wasn't hard to pick up what she'd actually been trying to do in the passing days. Especially when she was scheduling time away just to work on said project.

I brushed my hand over my head, still buzzed close, as I preferred it that way. It was easier, low maintenance, and I had enough to think about these days.

I folded my hands on top of my head. "She's wants to leave me that bad, huh?" I asked to no one, but I guess Tommy—his eyebrows flashed up in surprise. I folded my arms across my chest, shrugging. "I'm not stupid, Tommy. I know she's trying to use this to get out. If she's not trying to get a job with Roxie, she's obviously trying to get a good recommendation."

Which she could get with me, which she *always* could get from me because she had me. The woman had me readily available in her back pocket, at her knees if she wanted to...

And I fucking hated it.

I hated how she made me so wild like this, out of my head and completely without control. The whole thing made me feel powerless. Like I was slipping back to a place I didn't want to be, and reaching into my pocket, I sought my cellphone again. I needed to call her or something.

"She probably just doesn't want to be blackballed by another guy like you," Tommy said, frowning as he lowered his head. The words had been said under his breath, but as I was no longer on my phone and currently looking at him, his dark head of hair shot up.

"Mr. Chandler, I didn't mean—"

"What *did* you mean, Tommy?" Because if he had something to say about me... about *Cami* and me, I needed to know.

A deer in headlights, Tommy really didn't mean to say what he had. Clearly, he meant his words not to be heard, and biting his lip, his jaw moved. "Please don't fire me. I need this job."

Goddammit.

"Tommy, this is important, and you won't be fired. I know your boss. I can make sure that doesn't happen. Just tell me what you meant."

He breathed heavily. "It's not for me to tell. I only know anything because I saw you, her, and that guy. Her ex-boyfriend when we stopped in New York."

"What about the guy?" I asked, curious. I mean, he may have seemed like an uppity little priss, but he didn't immediately scream douchebag. I understood Cami's body language when he came around and she had asked me to play her boyfriend in front of him. I guess I did know something else about him.

He hadn't pleased her. I knew that because *I* had pleased her. He hadn't been able to give her what she needed, and that meant something was either wrong with him, the situation she was in when she'd been with him, or a combination of the two.

Why didn't I see that sooner?

My heart suddenly drumming with a new need to find her, I eyed her assistant. "Tommy?"

He cringed. "She's going to kill me. I did a little research after I asked her about that guy. She told me his name, admitted he was her ex, but a Google search told me the rest."

"The rest?"

He nodded. "He ruined her life."

Fourteen

CAMI

"Colton?"

I didn't want to use his room key, but I would if I needed to get in there and talk to him. My boss had a habit of sleeping at odd hours, and pounding on his guest suite again, I attempted to rattle his door down.

Where are you?

I pounded again. "Colton, if you're in there, I need you to open the door. Jesse took the rental car for some reason."

Which was hella inconvenient considering *I* needed the car. We booked it for any of us to use while we were in town, but what the hell? The concierge downstairs said a one Jesse Michaels checked it out. He apparently acquired the keys and took off with them, and I didn't know why. I could only gather he was joy riding as I always rented cars to Colton's liking. In this case, I'd gotten us a newly released Audi, and that alone should have sent off warning bells we wouldn't be the only ones driving it. Unfortunately for me, it was the wrong time for him to do that, definitely not now when I had a deadline I was trying to meet. I needed to be at the printers so I could overnight those designs to Roxie tonight.

I pounded again before reaching into my purse for Colton's room key. I didn't know what I'd see when I got in there. He could very well be between not one but two women. I'd found him that way before.

But not as of late.

Because he stopped all that right after that night he'd been with me. I knew because, despite myself, I mentally kept tabs on him and everything he was doing. He may have gone out, socialized on this tour when the occasion arose, but I figured mostly for something to do. He never brazenly brought girls around me, and really, at the shoot today had been the first time I'd even noticed him touching one.

Stop it, Cami.

I needed to stop it because not everything he did was my business, and putting the key in Colton's door, I pulled it up quickly. The lights flashed on, and I would have gone in if not for Tommy coming out of his own room on the other side of the hall. I had one nearby as well, actually right next door to Colton's.

"What's going on, Cam?" he asked me, his head poking out. "You looking for Mr. Chandler?"

"Yeah, Tommy. Exactly that. He let Jesse take the damn car for some reason. I told him I was taking time tonight, that I needed it."

Not that he ever listened to me, but I had and I did instruct Tommy to keep eyes on him.

Tommy merely bit his lip. "Uh, did you check the bar downstairs?"

Lord knew that Colton had no flippin' reason to be going and doing that. He fortunately hadn't had any incidents lately. Maybe because drinking when you're on a promotional tour to restore your image was the last thing he should have been doing. His hardest drinks were club soda, and I even made sure of that in his personal wet bars in the staterooms or suites he stayed in.

"Good idea," I said, pocketing the key. "If I can't find him, I'll have to get an Uber or something."

"Hopefully, it won't come to that," Tommy said, coming out. "It'll all turn out all right. Just keep calm. I know it will. Like I said, you deserve it."

I really didn't know why it took me so long to realize my assistant had become a friend sometime along my journey working for a sports star. I smiled at him before making my way downstairs to the lower levels of our hotel. In the heart of downtown, San Francisco had a nice nightlife, and the hotel we stayed in contributed to that. Wave had a cool aquatic feel to it the moment I set foot in it, people either dancing or relaxing, and fighting through the crowd, I realized finding Colton would be a feat in itself. He enjoyed environments like these, blended into places like this when I was the complete opposite. I stuck out with my modest dress when others sported croptops and stiletto heels.

Looking like I was actually going to a job interview instead of a bar, I attempted to make this visit quick. I scanned through the room for an obvious subject. Colton would have at least a foot over any man in this place, and considering most of the patrons I saw were female, I figured he'd stand out.

The women he'd been with today definitely did.

I spotted the cheerleaders from the shoot immediately, two of them in a pair. The other girls from the shoot weren't there, and these ladies must have decided to get some drinks. I honestly figured that's where they'd all be tonight, Colton with them.

I mean, he had signed their breasts.

I really didn't want to go over to them, but I figured they were my best bet regarding the whereabouts of my employer.

If they didn't know where Colton was at I'd do one more rotation before calling that Uber.

Preparing for that, I got my phone out, approaching the women. The girls were surrounded by other men, their long legs and miniskirts I was sure helping. I waved, gaining their attention, and funny enough, as soon as they saw me, they sprinted over.

"You girls seen Colton?" I asked them, charging my voice above the bar's energy. As people danced, I got bumped a little bit during my question.

The ladies crowded in. "You haven't seen Colton, have you?" one asked me, clearly not hearing my question over the music. The girl grinned with the reddest lips. "We asked him to come with us, but he said he was busy. That he had other plans."

"Other plans?" I didn't think I had him on the schedule for anything. But then again, other plans could mean personal ones.

The girl who spoke nodded. "Yeah, and he looked in a big hurry. Had Jesse get his car keys and everything."

Car keys...?

"It was such a bummer," the girl stated, frowning. "We were supposed to have fun tonight."

I didn't really care what that "fun" entailed, and clearly, I wasn't getting anywhere with these two. I quickly thanked them for their time before bowing out of the conversation. They let me leave only after I told them I'd mention their location to Colton or Jesse if I saw them. After being in this business for a bit now, I knew girls like this. They just wanted to be around these guys. Men like Colton and Jesse were a dime a dozen just as they were, two sets of people operating in the same world. Coming here, I planned to use some of that to my advantage after being shut out of NYC. My intention had been to build some connections and maybe work my way into the correct industry once people saw me for *me* versus who Taylor ended up making me out to be. A bug in people's ears, he spread his lies to whoever wanted to hear them.

"She's difficult to work with" or "she's very combative" came to mind, amongst some of the things I had to hear about my own self from other people. It'd actually been an old colleague to slip me the truth, to let me know what was going on in that world, and that I could no longer be a part of it. She wanted to give me a tip so I'd stop wasting my time.

The hurt of that day only resurfaced upon seeing Taylor, someone so arrogant to actually hug me the day he saw me. Getting angry all over again, I bumped into a person behind me.

"Tommy told me you came down here to look for me?"

It was amazing how it all worked. How thoughts of frustration and anger could melt away within moments of him being here. It honestly scared me how easily he'd been able to do it.

He gained in proximity behind me, and before I could turn completely, he let me see him.

Intense, blue eyes stared down at me, lean muscle pressed hard into the seams of his silk shirt and tan dress pants. He normally wore athletic shorts and muscular tees, but not today.

He put his hand out. "Want to dance with me, Cami?"

Why would he ask when there were others around? People could see us, but he didn't seem to care.

Dance with him. You want to...

"I'm working on that project for Roxie," I told him, fighting my urges. I backed away and hit another patron in the crowded bar. "I have to deliver the mock-ups tonight—"

"Already done," he admitted, then immediately slid his hands into mine.

I didn't resist anymore as he tugged me to him, pulling me into a dance.

He leaned in. "Dance with me."

He took the initiative, but didn't make me dance. I simply fell into it.

I couldn't fight it even if I wanted to do so.

We moved for a little while, slow before his voice fought its way into my head.

"I got your design to the printers," he said, squeezing my side. "Mailed them myself personally."

His words caused me to wake up out of the dreamlike state I'd been in. He'd brought me there so easily.

My lips parted. "You... You what? Why?"

I mean, how?

He did it himself...

It wasn't like him to go the extra mile, help me out. At least not as of late. I'd given him plenty of reasons to keep his distance from me, but for some reason he wasn't any longer.

Adjusting his firm hands around my waist, Colton caused my tummy to dance.

"Because it means a lot to you," he said, his expression serious. Bringing his head down, he brushed his cheek against my hair. "It means a lot to you."

He kept saying that a couple more times, and I got lost in the depth, his baritone voice that took me away. The pair of us had been so hot and cold with one another lately, moments like these so rare. Things only got hotter as his solid body pressed against my curves, my breasts stimulated by only a subtle brush of his solid chest. And then there was his smell, so inherently male he nearly inebriated me. I was drunk off him and the chill vibes of the bar.

I lay my head down against his chest with no power, complete submission to him. I was happy for this peace. I felt I'd lost him in these passing weeks.

"Cami?"

He broke my euphoric state but only slightly, his voice soft like the night he kissed me. The moment those thoughts arose, my thighs squeezed together. He hadn't kissed me on the lips. At least not the ones on my face.

I pulled myself from my mind, staring up at him.

"Why didn't you tell me about your boss, Camille?" he asked, scanning my eyes, and my stomach plummeted. He frowned. "The guy at the airport. He was your boss, right? Tommy told me you used to work for him."

Why would he tell him that? Embarrass me like that?

I started to pull away, but Colton braced my hand.

"Before you get upset, I made him," he said, his eyes serious. "But why didn't you tell me? Why, Cami?"

He brought me in before I could put anymore space between us. He wouldn't let me go. He refused.

And I was so grateful for that.

His hand came up, and he brushed his thumb along my cheek, catching dampness I hadn't known was there until he touched it.

"Cami..."

"I was afraid," I admitted. "I was afraid of..."

Him. I was afraid of him and being hurt again. Colton could be so much energy, fire, and warmth, and a girl could easily get lost in who he was. I'd seen many, and I couldn't be one of them, not after what happened to me.

My heart wasn't ready for it.

It wasn't ready for him and all that could be, so I shut him out. It didn't matter how I actually felt about him. It didn't matter that I...

A lengthy digit crooked beneath my chin, and when he stepped forward, he bent and pressed his mouth softly to mine.

So much heat drifted into my lips, our kiss, when he

parted my mouth and tasted my tongue. Warmth flourished in me completely at such a simple taste, the same from his hands when he brought them around my hips and pressed me against him.

"I'd never do that to you, Camille," he said, so softly as his lips pinched mine. He brushed my nose, his mouth fluttering along my lips. "You have to know that."

"I do," I said, shuddering beneath his mouth, his taste. I closed my eyes. "I was just scared."

I opened my eyes the same time he opened his, his fingers dancing in my hair. I didn't know what to make of his expression, his blond eyebrows drawing in.

"Scared of me," he said, swallowing. He turned away a little. "I'm a little scared of me too."

When his head lowered, I made him look at me, his mouth coming into my hand. I had no idea if anyone was looking at us. With the tightness of the bar, we could just be two more faces in the crowd or easily the object of a flash or shutter. For all I knew, we could show up on YouTube tomorrow.

But for some reason, I didn't care.

He didn't care either when he cuffed my wrists, letting me get closer.

"You can tell me anything," I told him. "About what you're going through? I know you said it was addiction and you're good, but..."

He had so many secrets, and he'd be foolish to think I, or others around him, hadn't picked up on that. The media had allowed him to let his struggles go and even Joe had for the sake of Colton's career. With their distance, his family maybe even sat unaware of the events that have clearly been occurring in Colton's life, but I was close. I was in the trenches, and if he needed someone, anyone... God help me, I would be there for him, this powerful man.

This man who was now shaking in my hands.

He kissed me hard suddenly, the rush of him pulsating through his lips. So intense, I felt those truths starting to form, that he was finally letting me in...

And letting himself go.

Fifteen

CAMI

"Cami..."

He'd spoken the words in my room, along my chest as he pressed me against the door. I think we came here because we couldn't even make the extra feet to his suite.

I slipped off my heels, dropping in height and making this man even mightier above me. His head bent, and mouthing my chest, Colton still stood more than a head taller than me. His wide frame caged me as I drew in a husky breath beneath his mouth. He pulled one of my dress straps as well as my bra away, tonguing the line where they'd both been.

"You're so beautiful," he said to me, the words sounding achingly true with his drawl. Needy, he reached up and cupped my breast, the subtle squeeze enough for me to pop up on my toes and grip his shoulder blades.

Planes of hard, muscled flesh simmered hot through his dress shirt. My hands danced down to his belt buckle, and he easily let me open it. A pair of toned legs revealed themselves the moment his dress pants fell down to his ankles, his bulge large and ready as it poked through his dark boxer briefs. After toeing out of his shoes, he removed his pants. He returned to me only in moments, and heading to the floor, he gripped beneath my dress.

Warm, wet licks accompanied the softest kisses to my thighs, and each inch of my dress Colton lifted was like a grant of permission to his mouth. He kissed me warmly, hotly, and when he pressed his mouth between my legs, I held him there.

"I want to do it again," he'd once said to me, doing so when he removed my panties, then brought my leg over his shoulder. Holding my bottom, he rocked me against his mouth, his tongue making me wetter than I already was.

I gripped his head. "Oh, God. Oh, God..."

He could make me come so easily like this, right here before we even made it to the bedroom. Neither one of us said where we were headed after he kissed me downstairs. We just walked, hand in hand, until we made it here.

Until we finally made it together.

So much of that wait had been because of me, my lack of trust and faith in him. Tonight, he not only helped me complete my assignment with Roxie, but ensured it. He said because it meant a lot to me. He hadn't meant enough to me, at least when it came to how I'd been treating him. He'd been nothing but kind to me.

He's not Taylor.

He wasn't and never would be, this man so full of his secrets. I wanted him to tell me, show me how he felt, and if I did one thing tonight, I could show him I not only trusted him but had faith in him too.

He squeezed me to him, taking deep and greedy breaths as he pleasured my sex. Shuddering, he actually groaned before dragging slow dips of his tongue between my folds.

"It's been too long, Cami," he said, sucking. He went for my clit and rose from his haunches to take me.

And then came his teeth.

Delightfully stimulating nibbles nearly brought me down

to my knees, and using my core, I wrapped my legs around his head. I rocked my hips into his face, using strength I didn't even know I had.

"Fuck, Cami. Fuck..."

He ate me—hard and didn't try to be gentle about it. He braced my thighs to his head and I doubted he could breathe with the lack of air I allowed him to have. My hips steady, I was just as greedy for his mouth as he was to please me. His tongue entering me, he used it to funnel my juices into his mouth, his body shaking beneath my legs.

"Colton..."

I mean, what else could I have said? This man was so hot and needy beneath me, wanting *me* when he could have anyone. He literally had everything he ever wanted, but in this moment, he was here in my room. He was with me, and overwhelmed by that, I allowed him to have me, to taste me in the ways he said he missed. My body shuddering, the fire in my belly came all too quick, but I didn't fight it. I wanted it to happen.

I wanted to come and only by his hand.

Colton slowed his tastes during my orgasm, bringing me down from the high like he had that night. Forcing my thighs apart, he made me widen for him, exposing me in ways I had never been exposed. He made me face him full on. He didn't let me hide.

"So beautiful," he rasped, kissing my mound. I hadn't shaved again, and his tongue danced along the hairs. I'd never shave again if he liked them.

Closing my eyes, my entire body felt numb. Like I couldn't do any more, standing a complete and total feat. I slumped, but he caught me, and before I knew it, he was on his feet and carrying me.

He cradled me like a damsel, so small in his large arms.

Placing me on the bed, he remained that massive guy, nothing on but his boxers and dress shirt.

Wanting to see him, I got up on my knees, unbuttoning a shirt nearly as sharp blue as his azure eyes. Those irises followed along with the movement of my fingers, observant and ready. Gripping my wrists, he allowed me to move his shirt down his powerful shoulders and back.

Golden flesh flexed and shifted with only subtle movements, Colton's body athletic perfection. He worked hard for his body, one of the hardest workers *I* knew despite what he said to me. Upon sliding his shirt away, his pecs jumped, brown nipples warm and hot under my hands.

He drew in a breath as I touched him, and shifting me on my back, he covered me.

"You're safe with me," he said, bending to capture my mouth, but before he could, I stopped him. I already knew I was safe with him, that he'd never do what my ex did to me.

"You're safe with *me*," I emphasized, reaching down to take his hand. I placed it over my heart while I touched his. "And you'll always be, Colton. Always."

I wanted to tell him something he needed to know, so many... trials I felt within this man. He seemed like he carried the weight of the world on his shoulders since that day, well, that day I found him.

He'd been in so much pain—and not just the obvious physical trauma. The war within himself I had seen in his eyes, and the fact he'd told me not to tell his family, the people he was the closest to in life, about what I walked into that night spoke volumes to me. He didn't want them to see that part of himself.

He didn't want them to see his pain.

I'd seen glimpses of it every day since, some days more than others, but it was always there at least a little. He was going through something, and whatever it was...

It made him hurt himself.

I could see the pain in his eyes just as well as I did on the days he let it slip, and when he took my hand from his heart, touching it to his lips, he closed his eyes.

"You see me..." he said, opening them. "You're the only one."

The shine in his eyes was definitely noticeable, but he closed them again before I could see it anymore. He pressed his mouth hard to mine, and that kiss, though just as warm and hot as before, held a desperation I'd never felt. It was like he was trying to find something in me.

Like he was trying to get *safety* from me.

I readily gave it, lifting my mouth for him to have. From before, I could still taste myself on his lips, and the combination of us set me off in ways I'd never experienced. He turned me on in so many ways, brought things out of me I'd never before seen, and I believed I did that for him too.

His boxers slid down his chiseled hips, his cock sharp and erect. Thick and full, he massaged its girth before letting me.

"It's yours," he said, pumping into my hand. "I'm yours."

His voice weak, vulnerable, he pushed his mouth onto my neck. He allowed me to hold him, stroke him, while he bowed his head in submission. He gave me all control, and I didn't know what to say.

"I do see you," I ended up saying, tasting his perfect lips. Opening them, he gave me even more access, holding me close before taking me with him when he fell to his back. There, he worked a toiletry bag open on his nightstand, pulling a condom out.

"Come to me," he said, sliding a condom on before bringing me forward. "And let me see you."

Warm fingers undid the clasp of my bra, and soon, I was just as naked as he was, exposed. In the dimly lit bedroom, neither of us did anything at first, just watching each other.

Colton's finger explored, his long digit traveling slowly down my body. He brushed my shoulder, my arm, and when he circled a nipple, I drew in a breath. He pinched one of them between two fingers, and at the same time, he brought me down on his cock.

"Cami..."

He said what I felt, our bodies completely right for each other despite his large size. I had womanly curves which could sustain his frame, and we easily met in the middle. His hips moved with intention, slow and not without purpose. He knew what he was doing, how to love.

"Let me see you, Cami," he repeated, making my eyes open when he touched my cheek. "I love to see you."

He loved to see me... His words were filled with something I felt deeply in my bones. He may not have said he loved me, but there was no mistaking how I felt. I think I loved my boss.

I wondered for how long.

My eyes rolling back, I felt that love, that pain so deliciously right between my legs. His cock full and deep, he filled me up and made me feel so many things. Taking me on my back, he drilled his powerful hips, making me call out for him. I couldn't help it, each word a pull from my lips. I felt so much love in my heart, and I wasn't surprised when I parted my lips.

"I love you, Colton," I said and couldn't contain the words because they felt right. I watched Colton's reaction to them. He didn't say anything, but he did slow a little, a hesitation in his body. All too quickly, it was gone, and before I knew it, he was kissing me.

His lips warmed, still no words said, but I wondered if I needed to hear them. He was telling me so much with his mouth, his body. Taking me to my peak, he didn't release my mouth. In fact, he kissed harder, faster, until I pooled around him so hard I didn't think calling what I'd done an orgasm was the correct word. It was so much more powerful than that, something deeper, and he held me as I cried out and shuddered beneath him.

He hadn't been far behind, almost waiting when his abs clenched, and his cock pulsed between my legs. Milking me, he made slow movements with his lips, his kisses lighter but just as heavy and weighted.

"Cami?" he questioned, and my heart leaped, wondering what he'd say next. I had told him I loved him, and though he didn't say it back, I had felt something from his end. It'd been passionate, fulfilled, and completely beautiful.

And it hadn't been sad.

But there was sadness now, deep in his eyes, as he stared at me. Like everything we just experienced was over, and he woke up.

It was as if he was letting it go.

"Colton," I said, reaching out to touch his cheek.

He grabbed my hand. "Will you stay with me?" he asked, unexpected. He kissed my palm. "Let me hold you tonight?"

The fact he felt he had to ask me hurt, but it didn't hurt me. I felt for him and only him.

What's wrong?

He didn't tell me, and I gave him my answer when I brought my arms around him and let him hold me. He obviously needed something from me much deeper than this.

I just wish he'd tell me.

Sixteen

CAMI

STIRRING, the buzz of a cellphone hummed me awake after what seemed like only moments of sleep later. It came from Colton's side of the room, a constant buzz, and turning, I realized I was still in his arms. A large arm wrapped tight around me. I was pressed to his chest, and he didn't want to let me go.

"Will you stay with me?"

He'd sounded so... desperate, and holding him close, I lowered my mouth to his chest. A warm heat flowed off him, his arm gripping me closer. The cellphone continued to buzz, but he didn't stir. I touched his face, his eyes closed with sleep.

He must be tired.

That was all I could gather and not wanting to wake him, I snuck out of bed to stop the phone. Naked, I toed over to his side of the room, grabbing his cell. Whoever wanted him could have him in the morning. He was tired, and lifting his phone, I went to turn it off and would have had I not seen the name on top.

Maggie.

Something made me read the start of the text message

string. Mostly because there were so many. They were all from one person, this... Maggie.

Colton, I'm in town. Can I see you...?

This woman obviously could be anyone and was none of my business before what occurred tonight between Colton and me. I put the phone down, but it buzzed in my hand before I could place it on the end table.

Colton, I need you.

The word *"need"* made my swipe my finger across the screen, and the rest of the text messages kept me invested. He had a full text message screen from this woman "Maggie," but the texts were pretty much one-sided. Things like *"Please call me"* and *"I'm sorry."* Basically, there was a lot of apologizing, but from this one woman and nothing from him. She seemed like a possible bug-a-boo, but curious, I scrolled up to the very top of the conversation to find his texts. Once I found them, well, they didn't stop.

Colton: Hey, it was good seeing you today.

Maggie: I'm glad we met. I'm glad I got to see you. You look so much like your poppa.

Colton: Thanks. Can I see you again? I'm so happy you contacted me.

Maggie: Of course. Anytime. Of course.

Several more, and my eyes were still reading, a long exchange dating back months...

Maggie: Thanks for getting lunch. I know you're busy.

Colton: No problem, and I'm never too busy. Always call, please.

Dating back a year...

Maggie: I meant to call you today. Got caught up, but I wanted to see you. Really I did, Colt.

Dating back a year and a half...

Maggie: Hey, Colton. You there? Missed you today. I'm so sorry I couldn't get out again.

Colton: It's okay. I just really wanted to see you.

Maggie: I know. Me too. I really did mean to, but I recently got evicted. Rent sucks in this city. My super kicked me out, the ass.

Colton: Where are you staying? Do you need help?

Maggie: I couldn't ask you that.

Colton: You didn't. I offered. Please let me.

This had been the first occurrence, the first money exchange between him and this woman named Maggie. He'd dropped an envelope in the mail for her, a PO Box listed in Dallas, Texas.

Maggie: Colton, did you send the money?

The second time...

Maggie: Thanks for the money again. It really helped, and of course I'll play you back.

The fifth time...

Maggie: Colton, it just might be easier if you wire the funds this time. The mail's been running slow and a transfer is instant. I can get to a Walmart if you can do it through Western Union.

Colton: How about I just set up a bank account for you? I'd hate it if you weren't able to pay your rent on time because of me. I've just been on the road like crazy lately, but I apologize.

Maggie: Oh, baby. Please don't do that. You're only helping me, and I'm so proud of my boy.

Her... boy.

The exchanges continued. The *money* continued as Colton set up a bank account in her name, calling it "Margret Applebee." Margret...

Maggie: Honey... I'm so sorry I wasn't there.

This wasn't the first of this woman's apologies for not being there, but this was the first time he hadn't responded. It'd been the first time he *hadn't* reciprocated, and I scrolled up, finding the exchange before.

Colton: I'm so excited you're coming down here. And don't be nervous. I'll talk to Pop before you come. It'll be cool.

Maggie: Colton... honey, your poppa doesn't want me there. I told you I could come for your draft party, but...

His draft party?

Colton: Don't... Don't bow out. You said you'd come, and I promise it will be okay. I'll make sure it is.

Maggie: What about your brothers?

Colton: They'll be happy to see you as much as I was the first time. They'll see you've changed. You've been sober, and they'll see that. They just need to see for themselves like I did. Please... Just come. I need you there, and I'll protect you.

Maggie: Okay.

Colton: Okay?

Maggie: Okay.

Colton: Thank you. It's going to be great. You'll see that.

But it wasn't great. It wasn't because she didn't show, and as I watched a woman plea to a perfect stranger, a man who wasn't this boy she spoke of, the anger rose in my veins. There'd been countless money exchanges, countless meetings over the course of a year and a half. Some of them were even during times I'd been with him. I traveled all over the world with this man, and during certain stops, he did go away. This woman seemed to always be there, lingering in the wind. Sometimes, he actually flew her out to where he was, to see him, and she came maybe one in five times he asked, usually after receiving money. Colton passed those absences off as being okay, and knowing him, I knew that to be true. Perhaps, it was okay. Perhaps, it was *fine* to give her money as long as she showed up to the last place he asked her to meet. His family held a *huge* draft party for him in Texas, the local politicians in attendance and everything. The entire city had basically been there, but one person who wasn't was Colton. I barely saw him at all during the entire party and, after it was over, even less. We got on the plane, and the first thing he did when we got back to LA was throw *another* party for himself. He disappeared after that, and the next time I'd seen him...

He'd overdosed.

Blinking, I pushed my hand over my mouth, so many texts after that moment. So many texts of "sorry" and how she'd heard about what happened on the news. There were so many texts asking if what he'd done had been because of her.

None of them were answered.

Little to her knowledge, Colton hadn't had access to his phone immediately after he ODed. *In the hospital*, he hadn't checked his fucking phone, and this woman would have known that had she come out to see him. The only people at the hospital were his family and me, no one else. I knew because I was there.

Maggie: I know you're in San Francisco. Please... if you can I want to see you.

So she was here now, was she?

Colton: Sure. I can meet you in about 30 min. Where do you want to meet up?

She immediately said for coffee in response to my text and that she'd be happy to see me, and I laughed. I just couldn't help myself. She wouldn't be happy after meeting me once she had to hear what I had to say.

And I'd make sure of that.

Seventeen

CAMI

I ARRIVED at the coffeehouse via our rental car, and I spotted the woman who'd been contacting Colton the moment I stepped inside.

Mostly because she was beautiful.

She'd chosen a table close to the cafe windows, easily spotted with her lengthy blonde hair and large eyes that took in the world. Currently, she had them honed in on the doorway I just walked in, her legs crossed and her wavy hair sitting on her shoulders. A few decades older than me, she had some years on her, but I only knew that from the age lines around her eyes and mouth. Time had seen those eyes, those features, and staring in wonder at her, I was easily fooled. I expected some kind of monster.

Mostly because that was how she'd been acting.

She'd treated Colton... cruelly, and I'd seen the evidence myself, a broken man who'd clearly wanted a connection to someone who only took advantage of him.

"Maggie?"

Eyes of a beautiful blue drifted toward me, so much like Colton and his brothers. I figured they got that from their dad as he was also blond and blue-eyed, a genetic trait. I guess between the pair, the men couldn't grow up *not* to be beautiful.

Maggie's gaze wandered, on the door, me, then past. She was clearly expecting someone else to walk through these doors, but if I had it my way, she'd never see Colton again. I was here to make sure of that. Her head rose as I approached her.

"Can I help you?" she asked me, uncrossing her legs, and without inviting myself, I took a seat at her table.

"Actually, yes," I told her, placing my bag down in my lap. I wanted it away from her, as I had good reason not to trust her. "You know my friend. Colton Chandler."

"Colton?" I watched her eyes simply light up at Colton's name, and if I hadn't known any better, the expression had been genuine. Maybe it had been, since the man clearly was her meal ticket. She sat up. "Where is he? Is he okay? I got his text."

Before this could go any further, I showed her that text on his phone I slipped away with. I left mine at the hotel with a note on it in case Colton woke up before I could return. I said he could call me on it and reach me if he needed. I just hoped I got back before he did wake up so I wouldn't have to explain the reason behind the switch.

Maggie's eyes twitched while gazing at the screen and her sight lifted to me when she sat back.

"I don't understand," she said, bracing her purse now. "Who are you? And where's my son?"

Her son... such a loose term she was using. As far as I knew, Colton only had one official *legal* mother. He had his stepmom, Ann, and a couple of other pretty awesome mother figures in his life. I knew for a fact his grandma Rose and aunt Robin raised him and his brothers from the time they were children. They raised them because *this* woman was completely absent from their lives. The reasons for her exit were unknown to me, of course, none of my business, but I summed up on my own a pretty good reason anyone would abandon their children.

Pure and utter selfishness.

My theory was only backed by the text messages I read. She was a manipulative woman who took advantage of someone who merely wanted to connect with her, and I'd say, if anything, desperately. He'd been desperate for a relationship with her, and she seized that glimmer of hope just as easily as she'd taken the handouts from him. She used him, hurt him, and if not for me, she might have actually killed him. Colton's heart had been too big, too open. It got him in trouble, and when it did, he'd had too much pride or whatever to ask for help. He needed help, someone to be there for him. That someone wasn't this woman, and I was going to make sure of that.

I put my phone away. "I read what was exchanged. The text messages between you and him?" I scoffed. "You know, he set up a charity in your name? He legitimately put aside money every month for you like the charity case you are, which I guess he had something there—"

"I don't have to explain myself to you. Whoever *you* are." She wrestled her purse on her shoulder. "The only person I need to talk to is Colton."

"Which you're not going to do. That is why *I'm* here for him," I said, standing up with her. "Do you know what you've done to him? What you put him through? He trusted you, lady, and what you did to him was sick, fucked up in every way."

"You don't think I know that!" she whisper-shouted, actually talking to me. She moved in. "You don't think I understand what I did. How he... How he hurt himself?"

So she really did know, something talked about in her text

messages. Colton overdosing had been all over the news nationally, not just here. Wherever she was staying at the time, she would have found out. Especially if he hadn't been answering her messages.

Shaking, the woman sank back down to her seat, her beautiful blue eyes haunted like she actually had seen Colton, *her son* foaming at the mouth and about to die. She hadn't seen that, only I had, and my tongue ticked to lay into her again. The only reason I held back was because she couldn't even see me. Her stare fell away into the cafe, lost.

"I was sick," she said, her lips trembling. She faced me. "I did use him. Like I use everyone, their dad."

Their dad...

"Blake was my first love," she said, shaking her head. "A wonderful man, and I took advantage of him too."

"Why?"

I knew for a fact Colton's dad was a hard-ass, but there was just something about him one could tell stemmed from nothing but good intentions. Nothing but *love* drifted off that man, and one could see that simply from the way he'd raised four boys on his own all while working himself. Today, their dad, Blake, not only had two professional athletes as a product of himself, but also two businessmen. Colton's brothers Brody and Hayden ran a furniture business alongside their creative father. They were all wonderful and successful people, and at the root of it all was that man, their dad.

Maggie swallowed hard. "Because I was sick, weak. I gave into the pressures of life. I don't know if Colton told you, but I had an issue with drugs, *have* an issues with drugs." She dropped her head. "They made it all easier, alcohol *made things easier*, and when I found out about Colton..."

"That's not him," I told her, not really knowing why. "He's not like that, not like you. He was just hurt."

She nodded her head, pushing back her hair. Considering

what she said about drugs, I'd actually been surprised since she look so together, but I guess some of us could hide it.

She cupped her mouth. "I left originally because I was no good for them all. They were better without me, better with just Blake, my mom, and my sister."

She'd left them all. I shook my head.

"Better for them," I said, nodding. "I supposed that's the easy way out, right? They're better and you can just go frolicking off in the night, doing whatever the heck you want."

"They were better." She brought her voice down again, and the sheen in her eyes was easily identifiable. She put out a finger. "You see what they've become. Colton, Griffin..."

"Then why not leave them alone? Why not stay away from them? Colton?"

"Because they were okay," she said, the cry clear in her throat. "They were older. They made it, and they didn't need me."

Her voice wavered on that last bit, her hands falling into her lap. She forced her fingers through her lengthy blonde hair, and though she hadn't continued, I picked up on where she might have been headed. She was right. They were older and didn't need her, but maybe that lack of need didn't go both ways.

This woman was clearly troubled, needed someone, and possibly, she sought to fulfill that with Colton. I had no idea if things started out genuine or what, but she obviously took things to a place they shouldn't have been taken, too much temptation with his successes.

Too much temptation for a sick woman.

"I didn't mean to take anything from him," she said, nodding. Tears fell away from her eyes as she lifted her head. "I honestly hadn't. I had been clean for a while, and then... I wasn't anymore. I lost my job. Things got hard again."

"And you took the easy way out."

Her lashes lifted. "I took the easy way out, yes, and went to the drugs again." She dampened her pink lips. "Colton begged me to go to Texas, see his brothers and his dad, but I wasn't ready. I just couldn't. I was in the rough of it and refused to come back into their lives like that. Colton had no idea I'd fallen back into drugs and the drink. I was sober when I reached out to him. I wouldn't have come to him any other way. I actually cut off contact from anything but text messages for weeks because I *couldn't* see him. I didn't want him to see me that way, my baby boy."

"Well, he isn't a boy," I corrected. "He's a man, and he deserved an explanation from you no matter how messed up you are."

"I know that now. God, do I." Her shoulders shook, her fingers dancing on the table. She looked up. "I went to rehab the same time they announced he did. I'm clean again."

"And now you're back for another crack at it? Do you realize how fragile *you* are right now? Let alone Colton. You came to him clean for however long, sober for what? A few weeks, and you're trying to rebuild those ties again?"

"I didn't come back for *me*." Her face filled with red. "I know what happened to him. I know what I've done, and I came back to make sure he's okay."

"Well, he's not," I told her, spelling it out. "He's far from it. He's hurt, distracted..."

And had so much pain I actually felt its physical presence when he'd been with me earlier. He had it all clamped up in this little Pandora's box, not to be seen or opened without special access. I felt, in a way, he was starting to open up a bit with me, and that had nothing to do with her. He may be on the road to healing, but he'd definitely shy away from that with any influence from this woman.

"He needs you to stay away," I said. "He's broken, fragile, and the last thing he needs is you."

Her expression chilled. "And you would know? Whoever you are?"

"I would," I said, standing. "Because unlike you, I'm one of the people who has been there. I'm one of the people who will *stay* here for the long haul."

As long as he let me, I would. I'd be there for him through this and anything else, because I truly loved him.

Picking up my bag, I pushed it over my shoulder. I put out a finger to her. "You will stay away from that man, and if I ever hear a whisper of you coming around him, well, you better lawyer up, baby, because I'm going to come down so hard and fast on your ass you won't know what hit you in the morning. There are grounds upon *grounds* of manipulation, blackmail, and all kinds of shit I can present to lock you up and throw away the key. You'll stay away, and if not for yourself..."

For him. Because if he mattered the most, she would. At least for now. I couldn't say where Colton would be in a month or even a year from now, but he was bound to be better off without any negativity from her in his life. From what she told me, the separation would be good for her too. She could figure herself out, come to things on her own terms, and maybe, one day, she would be better for him.

Maybe, one day, she'd be better for them both.

Today, unfortunately... tragically, wasn't that day for either of them, a son without a mother and a mother who obviously wanted her son.

I started to walk away but stopped at her voice.

"Can you at least tell him I love him?" Her voice got closer, like she stood. "Please..."

I closed my eyes, not sure if I could even do that. Maybe one day, but it was just too soon, too fresh. Quickening my feet, I made it to the door, but an obstacle in my way stopped me, a man big and broad, and I knew who he was before I even scaled up to his face.

I supposed I recognized his basketball shoes.

Colton had my phone in his hand, his eyes slightly red like he'd been torn from sleep, and maybe he had been. He slept so soundly with me in bed, but I knew for a fact he didn't sleep well normally. He told me. Tonight and the evening we spent together at his home had been a wonderful exception.

"Cami?"

I grabbed his arm, trying to push him out the door a little. "What are you doing here?"

"The 'Find My Phone' app," he said, sliding his arm away. "What are you doing here? And with my phone? Why did you leave?"

So many questions he had, and I would have been happy to answer them if not for who he clearly saw moments after his final question. I didn't even have to turn around to know he knew. His entire body language changed, his body stiffening after his gaze rose above me.

"Colton...?"

Again, I didn't turn, the voice of hope behind me in my ear. It'd been *her* voice, his mom. Instead, I chose to grab Colton's arm.

He took it away again, facing me instead of her. "What is she doing here? Why are you with her?"

This moment I actually chose to look at Maggie, that same hope in her eyes I'd heard in her voice. Purse in hand, she'd left the table, slowly making her way toward us.

She raised her hand, a wave. "Colton... baby—"

"I'm *not* your baby," he stated, lifting his own hands. The words so sharp, Maggie stopped in her place, cringing. She could do nothing as Colton chose to grab *me*, pulling *me* out of this situation and outside the coffeehouse. The door chimed when we left, and though no words were said initially on the street, Colton's eyes were wild.

He lifted his hands. "What the actual fuck? Cami, what—"

"Let me explain." Because he was freaking out, panicking. I grabbed his shaking hands. "Colton—"

"No. No!" He wouldn't even let me touch him, backing away when he pushed his hands over his buzzed head. "You went to see her? See my mom..."

He could barely even say the word and he shouldn't have. That woman was no maternal figure to him. He had plenty of those in his life, and none of them were her.

"Why?" he asked, a clear strain in his voice. "Why? Why? Why...?"

He kept asking that, making me cringe, and I wanted to explain myself. He was asking me to explain, but I found it hard by the way he was looking at me. Like I overstepped my position. Like I betrayed him when I hadn't. I'd only done this for him.

"Colton, I just had to talk to her. I wanted her to stop talking to you. I saw your text messages with her."

"You *read* my texts?" More of that betrayal, his irises flaring as he pushed those words through his teeth. "Why, Cami? Why?"

"Because you weren't doing it yourself," I explained, feeling I had to do so quickly. "She was coming back again, trying to lead you down a path. She was trying to hurt you, Colton, and I just—"

"Were what? Trying to protect me?" His jaw clenched. "Why does everyone feel like they need to fucking protect me all the time? You, my brother, and my goddamn family all the *fucking* time. You know, Griffin came down here to tell me she might come? And that was after he felt like he had to step in to make sure Miami stuck with me."

"Because he cares about you, Colton," I said, trying to calm him down. "We all care. We all love..."

I couldn't finish when his attention flashed to me, his head turning like he couldn't take it.

Like he didn't *want* me to finish.

For some reason, he didn't want me to say I loved him, even though I had before. It bothered him for some reason, and my insides caved like I'd been run over by one of the buses in the street.

Shaking, I cradled my arms. "I care about you, Colton. I just wanted to help."

"Well, you didn't," he said, closed off as well. His hand folded behind his neck. "You didn't, and you may have only made things worse. I was handling the situation with her. I was dealing with it."

"Ignoring her isn't dealing with it." I tried to find his eyes. "You have to be clear with her what you want."

"Like you were with me?" His words cut. "When you didn't want to be with me because of your ex? You were pretty damn crystal clear about that, weren't you?"

I cringed. "You're just lashing out, taking this out on me because you're hurt. Don't." I paused, trying to keep my breathing even. "Don't push me away. I just want to help."

"I don't need your help, Cami—"

"I don't want you to hurt yourself again!"

The words vibrated through the open air like lightning, our reality. They severed through the world like a turbulent storm, and the pair of us were in the middle of it.

Colton's lips trembled, his breath a harsh rupture raising his chest.

"You think," he started, squeezing his eyes before looking at me. "You think I hurt myself on purpose?"

He... honestly didn't see it? What he'd done because of that woman?

I shook my head. "You overdosed after all this shit with your mom."

"Because I was stressed," he admitted. "I got fucked up because of a fucked-up situation. That *doesn't* make me suicidal, Cami."

"Okay." I raised my hands because I didn't want him to shut me out, walk away, but all that did was make him tense up.

His eyes narrowed. "Don't look at me like that."

"I'm not."

"But you are." He stood back. "You're looking at me like I'm crazy, and you've once again assumed something about me."

I had assumed something about him, but the difference was this wasn't a snap judgment. He was a drug addict without a drug problem.

But for some reason he didn't know that.

He wasn't *aware* of what was going on, and I didn't know how to help him. I tried to approach him, but he wasn't letting me.

"I need space from you," he said, stabbing me right in the chest with the words. He shot a finger back to the coffeehouse. "And I need to go deal with this." He left me in the street after that, all those words between us. He wouldn't let me help him.

How could he when he didn't know he needed help?

Eighteen

COLTON

My mom backed into the cafe when I returned. Because she'd been watching. She may not have heard the fallout between Cami and me since she was inside…

But she'd seen everything.

I had always wondered what Maggie would look like when I saw her. I mean, I'd seen pictures of her, but with the stories my brothers shared about her over the years, I figured she'd be all drugged out. She'd be all frizzy hair and unkempt and with eyes bloodshot to hell. I figured a drug abuser would be clearly seen, and if she had been that way when I first met her, that would have made this whole thing easier.

She looked… put together then, as she did now. Like a real mom with a little sporty bag and summer clothes like the locals strutted around here wearing. She looked like… Momma, and that made things so much damn harder. I didn't want her to look like my *mom*. I didn't want her seeming a fraction of anything I concocted in my head of what the woman who gave birth to my brothers and me looked like, but she did.

She fucking did.

And she used that. She used every absent memory I had and created new ones every time we'd been together. We met up numerous times, spoken on the phone countless more, and our text messages were in the hundreds. They'd been every day with only hours passing in the beginning. It'd only been too easy for her to disrupt my life and make me lie to everyone about her. I knew none of my family would be okay with her being around, but I was willing to do the hard stuff to prove to them that she should be.

I did do the hard stuff in the end.

The fact that I labored so hard actually sickened me now, and she stood back when I came in. A clear shock and awe moved in her eyes at seeing me, and what lingered beneath the surface only pissed me off. It was a look I knew I'd sported many times before upon seeing her, a happiness deep within, and I didn't want her to be fucking happy. I wanted her to suffer, to have as much pain and agony as I carried every day since the last time I spoke to her. It'd been the day she bailed on me when I'd been her biggest champion. That incident and more made me push Cami away just now, and I only resented her more.

"Colton..." More of that fucking hope in her voice. She swallowed. "You came."

"I'm going to make this quick with you," I said, knowing both my body and voice were shaking. She brought me to a place of little control, and I hated her for that.

I hated *her*.

Breathing, I attempted to force the shakes out, alleviate the nausea and everything else that threatened to rupture at being forced to confront this woman. I strained my mind to the brink, my body to the edge, like I had every game I played on the court, but this time, the effort wasn't as easy to overcome. This wasn't a game. This was my *life*, and the stakes were so much higher. I was in a dark daze so hard to get out of.

She approached—slowly.

"Colton, if I messed things up," she said, hesitant. "Between you and your friend? I'm sorry. I didn't mean for that to happen. She clearly came here without you knowing, came here for you?"

For me...

And the fact that she regarded Cami as my friend only cut my insides apart even wider, like I couldn't gain air. Like my lungs were too big for my chest and the cave inside physical pained.

I breathed deeply, facing Maggie.

"That woman I sent away?" I questioned, physically quaking. I dampened my lips. "I love her. She's the only woman I've *ever* loved outside of members of my own family, and what's worse is I couldn't even share that with her tonight. I couldn't tell her that I loved her back when she told me because I'm so fucking screwed up by everything I've been through with you."

The words sucked the air out of the room, Maggie's hand going to her mouth, and hearing them aloud, put a number on me too. My stomach knotted, the nausea surfacing again.

Maggie's eyes glassed. "Colton..."

"No," I said, shaking my head. She got enough words in the past—it was my turn now. I put my hand to my chest. "You know I can't make decisions? That I follow everything everyone else does to a simple food order, or juggling women I don't even care about because I don't trust myself? Because I don't believe in my own decisions enough to make them. I question *everything* about myself every day because in the back of my mind I think, will this make me like her? Will it send me down a path I don't want to go down and push everyone I've ever cared about away in the process?"

Tears dripped through her eyelashes, but I didn't care. She had enough, had enough of me, and she was about to know it.

"Basketball and Cami were the two decisions I've ever really truly held faith in," I said, nodding. "And I just barely held onto one and might have lost the other entirely—both because of you—and I'm not doing it to myself anymore."

"I never wanted that," she said, coming to me. "I just wanted you to be okay. I wanted all of you to be okay. You and your brothers? Things got hard for me, Colton. They were hard, and I couldn't be there for you. I wanted to come to your draft party. I wanted to be there, but I fell into some old habits."

Meaning... drugs, and I'd be naive to say I hadn't suspected. The fact only made me more like this woman than I ever truly wanted to admit. I turned to drugs too when I had been messed up, something I never touched.

I backed away. "Tonight is the last night I want to hear from you, and that means my brothers and their families as well. Griffin told me you came for him, his wife, Roxie?" I shook my head, disgusted. "You needed money? Really—"

"No." She dared to come close to me. "I went to Griffin, to his wife *only* because I needed to know about you. You wouldn't talk to me, Colton, and I was worried."

"Worried." I nearly spat the words. "Because of you, the woman I love thinks I'm crazy. She thinks I tried to hurt myself over you."

I was rattled, mostly by this, her words and how she looked at me. I couldn't face her again even if I wanted to. I was too angry, embarrassed, too...

I forced the emotions away. "Stay the hell away from me."

"Colton—"

"I mean it!"

The whole room went silent, the coffeehouse, everything.

That's when I saw the camera phones.

There were people with their phones out, all on us, and I

wondered for how long. My drama was now out in the air, my life messed up even more, and all because of this woman.

I threw myself through coffeehouse doors. I said all I needed to say and had my own battles now. I wanted to drink, dive back into the depths.

I guess I was more like her than I thought.

Nineteen

CAMI

We ended up leaving San Francisco separately, but not because I wanted to do so. Colton arranged for Tommy and me to be escorted home by other means, as he himself headed back home to LA last night. I only knew because a member of his security woke me up with the information that next morning.

He left me, left the situation, and knowing San Francisco was the last leg of his redemption tour, he had the freedom to do that. He literally didn't need me until he requested something of me, and finally, getting back into town, he didn't. He didn't call me, text, or anything.

I knew because I waited.

I'd been staying in a hotel for over a week, waiting patiently for him to come around, but the only thing that ended up coming in was a text from Roxie. She wanted me to come down to Miami, talk to me about the presentation I sent her. She liked it and, well, wanted to discuss.

I supposed that's what I wanted, right?

I knew this was big because she even arranged for me to fly down. She said it would be a quick trip, and she was excited to talk to me. I wanted to share the same, but there was so much on my heart. I did agree to go, though, and even texted Colton where I'd be in case he needed to get a hold of me. I got no response on the way to the airport and nothing after I finally landed. This hadn't surprised me, but I still hoped. I guess I was waiting out for a miracle, which I didn't get during my trip to Roxie's office, Rox, Inc.

It was a beautiful place when I got there, a beautiful space with sparkling floors. The bright chandeliers brought attention to the glistening floor tiles, and the sound of clicking heels surrounded me the moment I arrived. The staff was ninety percent female, a powerful essence to the place, and the main source of it came in the form of the CEO. Roxie was in the business of helping people, athletes in particular, and I stood the moment she arrived in the lobby.

In her white power suit, she approached me, just as show stopping as the rest of her team around her. They buzzed like busy bees. Working for a cause like this was my dream. I came to NYC, wishing for the same, but I'd gotten involved with someone who ultimately took any opportunity I could possibly want away from me.

How ironic personal involvement got me here as well, to this place...

"Ready?" Roxie asked me. She was ready for her two o'clock—me—and I pretended like I had it as much together as she did.

Portfolio in hand, I put my hand out for hers and gave a strong shake, but I'd be lying if I said my mind wasn't on other places. I kept my thoughts of Colton and everything else on the back burner, making my mind stay here.

Once in Roxie's office, the doors closed behind us. Roxie moved behind her large desk, and I took the front. She brought me into her world, and I was ready to listen.

The pacing of the meeting moved quick, and I had to stay

on my toes just to keep up. Roxie had been completely prepared. She'd already had my concept boards set up and everything. She had them brought in during the meeting, and she'd taken the liberty of making mock-ups of where they'd go. An illustration of my design was set up over a highway. Right downtown in the heart of Miami.

"I want you to come and work for me full time," she said to me, concluding with *that*. "I think it'd be a match made in heaven actually."

I did too. This place... was ultimately perfect for me.

"Of course, we'd have the issue of your boss," she went on, eyeing me with a coy grin. "Colton says he's okay with giving you up, but I'm not exactly sure why."

She had my attention more than she already did.

"You..." I started, my mouth dry. "You spoke with him?"

Her nod was firm. "I did, and he said he's okay with you working for me, coming here, but I find that hard to believe. Your work is amazing, and I have a feeling that's the case in everything you do. I'm finding it hard to believe he'd ever give you up."

The words twisted a dagger in my gut. Though I knew that wasn't her intention. She was just trying to make me feel valued, nothing more.

"I guess he's allowing me to move in another direction," I supplied, saying the words actually making me nauseous. I hadn't been ready to let go of him.

He'd apparently been ready to let go of me.

I forced a smile. "If he's okay with it, then, yes, I'd love that. I'd love to work here for you."

Roxie folded her fingers together, tilting her head. "Well, I'd be happy to have you. I can have my legal team start drawing up papers for your contract immediately, full benefits, and you'd have your own office. It's right next to mine actually."

More than perfect. I nodded, trying to be confident in the way I presented it. The pair of us ended our meeting with not just a handshake, but a hug, and I hadn't been surprised. Roxie just seemed like that type of person, genuine in her overall demeanor. In a way, I felt as if she was inviting me to be a part of some type of family she'd established here.

"You should come to lunch with us," she said, opening the doors for me. "I'm sure he'd love that."

The "who" I didn't get to ask about until it was too late.

Colton stood there, his body swole and thick in the Under Armor, paired with athletic shorts and sneakers he'd chosen to wear that day. It seemed he'd come right from the gym and to Roxie's office.

Seeing others with him, I soon figured out why.

Roxie's office was filled with men, *tall* and *blond* men, one of which was her husband, Griffin. He too wore shorts and an athletic tee, and his golden locks were slick and filled with sweat. The other two men I recognized as their older brothers, Brody and Hayden. Hayden, the oldest, was the most svelte of the men, his long hair pulled back into a ponytail, and the final brother, Brody, wore a backwards baseball cap on his head. The man was massive, like a literal freight train. He had a basketball under his arm, and all four men seemed to be involved in their own conversation in the middle of the office.

At least, until I arrived.

The youngest of them spotted me immediately, his lips parting. If he'd known I was invited to lunch with apparently *most* of his family, he sure didn't act like it. He stood there, jaw slack, and wasn't the first to make a move. That honor went to Griffin, who as soon as he spotted his wife, made only about three lengthy steps and arrived in her presence.

"Hey, babe," he said to her, pulling her close. He gave Roxie a modest kiss on the cheek, then cradled her close. The others joined us at this point, but Griffin's proximity didn't give them much access. It seemed the largest of them, Brody, hadn't cared about that because as soon as he made to it Roxie, he was grabbing her.

"Sister-in-law!" he said to her, spinning her around and making her laugh. He set Roxie on her feet. "It's been too long."

"It'll be longer if you don't give me my wife, Brody. Jesus," Griffin chided, but he did so with a smile, before taking Roxie's hand. Roxie gave him a nudge for that and let him go so she could give Hayden a hug.

"Hey, sis," Hayden said to her. Not as abrasive as Brody, he merely gave her that small embrace before drawing back. "How have things been?"

"Good. Just finishing up with Cami," she said, acknowledging me. "You guys apparently had fun."

"The most," Brody cut in, actually bouncing his ball in her office, which made Griffin shoot him a stern look. Brody shrugged. "Lighten up. You'd think you were the oldest."

"Someone needs to act like it sometimes," Griffin said, and all that did was make Brody jostle him. He replaced the ball with Griffin's neck when he slung his arm around him. The large men jokingly tussled for a bit, and all the while Colton stared at me.

It was like he was in a trance. He didn't move, and not even the fake scuffling of his siblings could bring him out of it. He stood stark still, and it was Roxie's voice that brought him to awareness.

"I hope you don't mind, but I invited Cami to have lunch with us," she informed them, touching my shoulder. "It seems she's accepted my offer to work for me, so we're all going to be seeing a lot more of each other."

This got a small round of applause from the big men, mostly Brody, who was obviously the jokester. The one who *didn't* clap was Colton, and for the first time since he'd seen me, his attention flittered away. He may have approved of me in regards to my previous employment, but at the present, he didn't express the same excitement as his brothers.

"Hey, I thought Cami worked for Colt," Brody stated.

Colton's eyes blinked wide. Suddenly, the attention was all on him, and with it, he was forced to acknowledge it.

Colton faced me. "She's been given a better opportunity. I'm happy for her."

He may have said the words, but they sounded more than empty. I didn't want to be here in this moment, and *he* clearly didn't *want me* to be here with him. What happened the last time we'd seen each other still held a weight between us, and that was so obvious *between us*. I'd been about to excuse myself until Colton did the honor.

"Hey, I got to go over some things with Cami," he said to the men. "See you guys outside?"

It'd been a crafty thing to say, keeping it more than casual, since I still worked for him. He could take me outside and tell me I wasn't invited there. Not that I was taking Roxie up on her offer for lunch. The man clearly didn't want me there, and I didn't want to be if I wasn't wanted.

Colton's brothers gave him each a handshake/hug combination when he lifted a hand in the air. He gave Roxie a hug, something he hadn't done in their initial greeting, then did in fact take me outside. We went out back behind Rox, Inc., apparently the perfect place to dismiss me. We ended up in a back parking lot, no one there but us.

"You're in town with your brothers," I concluded. It'd been something I didn't know, not that he'd tell me.

He watched the door. "Uh, yeah. My gram's birthday's next week. They're planning a party for her. Anyway, it was Griffin's idea."

"It was a good idea," I said. It was sweet and something a

member of the Chandler clan would do. It was something *Colton* would do.

His jaw moved, and the way he stared at the door was like he willed it to stay closed. It made me feel even more out of sorts, like I wasn't wanted.

I threw my hand in my hair. "I didn't know you'd be here. Roxie called me to Miami for a meeting. I texted you about it."

And he didn't respond to said text.

His gaze slid to me. "I know, and I knew you might be here, that it was a possibility."

"Well, don't worry. I won't ruin your fun. I was going to tell Roxie no to lunch."

He nodded, and there really was all still that between us. How had things been so good, so passionate between us and suddenly gone? It was as if it never happened, that he never cared about me or wanted anything to do with me. It made me angry, frustrated, and I faced the dark sky.

"I take it nothing was said to your brothers or Roxie," I said, looking at him. "You guys look chummy. I suppose your mom was never brought up—"

"No." He honed in, and I noticed he watched that door again. Why did he feel the need to keep so many secrets from everyone? What did he possibly have to hide where he couldn't let anyone in, where he couldn't let *me* in...

I breathed hard. "Colton—"

"Look, Cami. I gave you what you wanted, okay? You got your job. You got everything—"

"But you," I said, making him swallow hard. "I did get everything, but I never asked for it. The one thing I asked was you, for *you* to..."

Emotion filled the words and made finishing them impossible. They were impossible, this complete conversation hopeless.

"I need to go," I told him. "Give you your space like you asked."

That was what *he* wanted, so I was giving him that. His eyes closed at what I said, but he didn't argue with me to stay. He let me go.

"Cami," I heard him start to say behind me, but when no steps followed me, I continued.

I was lost in a sea of emotion, coming to the full realization of something. This was over, he and I were over. He was letting me go, and if it was so easy for him, I had to do the same. I made it to my rental car, but something told me to turn around. Something physically pulled me to do so, and the moment I did, I was glad. Colton was on the ground.

And he was holding his chest.

He was literally hunched over, and I ran, dropping all my things in the parking lot.

"Colton!" I screamed, reaching him. I grabbed him and he seemed lost when he looked at me.

He reached for me, a gasp in his throat. "Cami?"

"Colton, what's wrong? Colton..."

"Something... Cami, something's wrong. I can't... I can't see."

He stared at nothing, looking toward me but not at me. He held my hand, but he clearly couldn't see me.

"Cami? Cami?" He just kept saying my name, gripping my hand like he did so for dear life. "Cami, help me. I can't see." He really couldn't, staring at me blankly.

I screamed in that parking lot, calling out for someone, anyone to help me.

"Please, we need help!" I called again, staring down at this beautiful man. "Colton, stay with me, okay?"

"Cami..."

"Help, please! Anyone!"

"Oh my God. Colt!"

Colton's brother Hayden bounded toward us, the troops behind him. Brody, Griffin, and Roxie had been walking, but as soon as they saw me in the parking lot with Colton, they ran too.

"What's happened to him?" Hayden asked, getting to us first. With the other men, he moved Colton out of my arms and onto his back. Laid out on the concrete, Colton's back bowed suddenly off the ground, and alarm in his eyes, Hayden threw his hand out. "Someone call 911. Now!"

911... The number and the operator were still so clear in my head.

"Can you tell me what you think he took..." she'd said, but he didn't take anything this time. I know that. He was clean.

I'd been with him.

"I got it," Roxie said, suddenly on the phone. She called 911 while the men's attention stayed on their brother.

"He said he couldn't see," I informed them, my heart hurting. So much was like that day I found him. So much, but this couldn't possibly happen again. He'd been fine before. He was fine, until I turned my back and walked away.

"They said ten minutes," Roxie announced, hanging up her phone, and in all the panic, everyone was trying to get through to Colton. They were talking to him, asking him what was wrong and what could they do. He didn't answer any of them.

"Cami?"

He called for me, just like he had that night, and the world stopped with that word.

I was there immediately, and all too quickly, the others allowed me in.

I took his hand. "Colton, I'm here."

Something happened when he heard my voice, felt my hand in his. He squeezed, and suddenly his breathing wasn't so rapid, his vision no longer unfocused. The clarity formed in his eyes and, with their observation, the calm to his body.

He stared at me, and the world, his family, saw him come back to us. He came back to *me*, and so many jaws were dropped.

"What's happened? Was it a seizure?" Roxie asked, and as Colton's brothers probably didn't know, they said nothing. They only looked at me, and ironically enough, I felt I might have been the only one who had the answers. Something like this had happened to me before.

My heart moved.

"A panic attack," I rationalized, certain of the fact when Colton closed his eyes and let me guide him back. His breathing leveled out, and when it did, he gripped my hand so hard I thought he'd never let go.

"How do you know?" It'd been Griffin to ask, the others to wait. They might have waited forever if not for the flashing lights and the sirens pulling around the corner. They came for Colton and saved me from admitting the reason I knew the difference between a panic attack and a seizure. I knew because I'd seen Colton have a seizure.

It was way different from my panic attack, which initially brought me to LA.

Twenty

CAMI

There was something about secrets, the lies we told ourselves solely for our own protection. It wasn't something we necessarily did on purpose. It was like the mind's safety mechanism. We triggered it, and we were whole. We were safe.

Until we weren't.

It took my panic attack in NYC to let me know that. It took until I was on the floor, crying and alone with no one else in my corner for me to see what I allowed my secrets and my lies to do to me. I kept the secret inside that things were okay with Taylor, that how he was treating me was okay. So later, when I was railroaded with what he'd done to me and my career, it completely broke me down, I lost it all. And even though he had been the one to take it, I had been the one to accept it. I stayed in that city too long before demanding for a fresh start for myself, and it was only after I did that I started to get my life back. I got a man, a wonderful one who I felt like I should have seen. Colton said when we made love that I saw him.

But I didn't always.

He suffered with the stress about his mom for a long time before I found out. He had his own secrets, and like me...

I supposed he had to own up to them.

Twenty-One

COLTON

It was a different treatment center this time, and my doctor at the hospital advised it. I'd been diagnosed with a panic attack, and that was easy, right? It was easy to write off to my brothers, Roxie. They'd been freaking the fuck out when it happened, but the moment the doctor came in, told us what had happened, and gave me the all clear, the stress I thrust upon my family went away. Panic attack... fucking easy. I could write that one off and did at first. It was stress. *I* was stressed. I was about to play for a new team, changing the entire dynamic of my life, and the relief of a "stressful" diagnosis provided an easy out for my brothers, Roxie, and even myself. The rest of our family was informed, of course, but not with urgency or worry or the dire need for help. Hayden had been the one to make the call to Pop, Gram, and Aunt Robin, and the crazy thing was, he didn't even sound upset by it. He'd said I was stressed, had an incident, and after he assured my family things were okay, I didn't even hear from them. They'd trusted Hayden and what he was saying.

I'd been cleared.

The only person who wasn't confused, who didn't play

along with the game, was the woman who brought me back. She'd been with me *again*, and she didn't fall for the bullshit. Cami stuck around after the diagnosis, after my brothers and Roxie had left. She stayed, and I had to own up to my truths, those eyes that did see me. She knew something was wrong, and she said so before.

The doctor advising treatment only confirmed it.

I wasn't to go to a center for drugs and alcohol, no, but something else. He'd said I was depressed...

Depressed.

I'd never used such a word to describe myself, and even after the doctor told me, I still really didn't think I accepted it. I was just going through stuff, right? Stressed, and I intended to get help only because of the woman who stuck by me. Cami was there with the paperwork. She was even there packing my bags. She came with me on this "special" trip, and I suddenly found myself back on the other side of the country. The mental health center was a few hours outside of LA, and once dropped off, I had to do the next part alone.

"Just try," Cami said to me, kissing me once before leaving me with my bag. She had other things to tend to, excuses to make up for my family. I'd have to miss my gram's surprise party in order to commit to my stay here.

And so there were more secrets.

I intended to take them to my grave, and those first few weeks in the treatment center, surrounded by palm trees and nature, were a lot like my time at Shining Hope. I barely participated in anything, went along with the show. It wasn't until a few weeks in that something changed. I'd gotten a call to my room that someone came to see me, and when I went downstairs, I didn't expect anyone but Cami. She was the only one who knew I was here, getting help. Even my agent, Joe, believed I was simply on vacation. He handled all the business stuff and everything, giving me time to unwind. I'd fed him a story like everyone else.

I went to the arrival doors after that call to my room, fully intending to tell Cami that this wasn't working out, wasn't for me, but at the sight of another, I stopped in my tracks. My pop stood there, my... pop.

And he was here to see me.

～

We stared at each other for a while, he and I. A big man, he was wearing shorts and a button-up, his hands in his pockets, with the landscape behind him. We were both in sunny California, and the treatment center had big windows. They completely let the day in, making this place mellow and beautiful. It'd been the only thing that resonated with me while being here, the peaceful and calming environment. There were no cellphones, no distractions or people.

I stepped forward into the lobby where my pop was standing. He shouldn't be here. He shouldn't *know* I was here at all.

"Pop?" The word sounded weird, weird here where I shouldn't be seeing him, and at my voice, his expression fell. He looked sad, his blond eyebrows drawing in. My pop used to be stressed all the time and wore that stress all over his face in the past. But something happened only a few years ago. He stopped working so hard upon doing something he loved, and also found the love of his life in my stepmom, Ann. He was happy all the time now, and it'd been so long since I'd seen him frown.

He was doing so at me as I came forward, and when his lips parted, he sighed.

"Wanna go for a walk?" he asked me, not saying why he

was here or anything. He was always a man of few words, so when he spoke, a guy tended to listen to him.

I nodded at him, going along, and he strode through the center like he ran the place. After only a few directions from me, suddenly, we were out back in more peace, more environment. The butterfly garden surrounded by koi ponds was a great place to just walk, peaceful just like the rest of this place. I took my pop back there, and we did what he asked, walked.

We strode side by side on cobblestone trails, and the only time words were shared was when I pointed things out to him. He liked to know about nature, took us camping all the time as kids, and I let him know about the various plants and things. It helped the pair of us communicate, and I found myself really happy, at ease since being here. Eventually, we took seats in front of one of the koi ponds, and my old man hunched over, staring at them.

"You're a long way from Texas," I said to him, opening that door. I sat back and just... looked at him. My pop didn't like to travel, *hated* heights and planes, and yet here he was.

He grunted a little at what I said, acknowledging me. His hands rubbed together, and he nodded his head. "Thought it was important," he told me, leaning back. "And it took a lot to get her to tell me where you were, so don't be mad at her none."

My frown was on him when he faced me. My lips parted. "Cami?" I asked, feeling my heart leap a little. She was the only one who knew I was here, getting help.

Pop nodded again. "I called to check up on you," he said. "Felt like something was wrong."

"Why?" I'd been... so good at hiding it. I hid it even from myself. I didn't want to admit things weren't working right with me.

His jaw moved. "You used to shine, son." He faced me. "And you haven't done that for a long time. You don't come home, don't come to see us." His breath slowly blew from his lips. "Why didn't you tell us you were here?"

I said nothing, and unable to look at him, I stood. I never did things like that, walked away from a conversation with my pop, but I couldn't take it.

"I'm handling it," I said, thinking he wouldn't hear me, and I was talking to myself. I didn't want him to hear *any* vulnerability in my voice, but when his hand touched my shoulder, I knew he had. He was standing there, close...

And he wasn't going anywhere.

His other hand came to my shoulder. He squeezed them both, and I had to lower my head. I couldn't face him. I *knew* there was too much emotion going on inside me and he'd see it.

"You shouldn't have come," I forced out, that emotion fully charged in my goddamn voice. I breathed hard. "You shouldn't be here."

"What's going on, Colt?" he asked me, and I shook. I was *shaking*, and I knew he felt it. I *knew*. "Come on, son. Just... talk to me."

Talk to him. Talk. To. Him. I didn't talk to him. I didn't talk to *anyone*. I handled things myself. I dealt with it all. I had to because I was the youngest and I needed them to see that I could, but in that moment, my pop here and all my vulnerabilities around me...

I was tired. I was so goddamn tired and sick to death of feeling so vulnerable. I was done feeling like this.

I was done trying to admit I didn't need help.

"It's Momma," I confessed, turning. My jaw moved, my eyes hot. "It's been Momma for a while."

I didn't know how long it took to tell my pop about my mother coming to me. I didn't take in the reality of the amount of time it took to rehash almost two years of constant struggle. It'd been a struggle I took on all by myself and felt alone for so long. By the time I was done, it was evening and the twinkling garden lights started coming on. Pop and I were alone, had been for a while without a passerby, and not once did my pop interrupt me during my story. Not once did he look angry or disappointed. He just listened to me.

And that felt good.

Toward the end, he reached out, squeezing my shoulder. I thought he was going to tell me it was time to wrap things up, as my pop was never an emotional guy. He didn't wear his emotions on his sleeve.

But with his hug, he did.

He *hugged* me, something only I used to initiate as a child. I didn't hug him as an adult. He just wasn't a hugging man. He took care of us, loved us, but the hugging was usually Gram and my aunt Robin.

He was doing it now, hugging me tight and close, and I couldn't even react, in shock.

Mostly because I needed it.

I needed him and this moment and just to get it all out. I needed to realize I wasn't alone.

And that I never had been.

Twenty-Two

CAMI

It took him some time, a lot of time actually. Colton had a lot to work through and only he could do it. He didn't come back home when we originally thought he would. In fact, he stayed in treatment for several more weeks past the thirty-day commitment he made. He stayed because he felt he had to do so.

He stayed for himself.

Every day wasn't easy in the months that followed, but each one got better and better. Colton had to fall into his vulnerabilities, and after everything was out on the table, things with his mom out in the air, he was able to heal from it all. He told his entire family about his mom coming back and actually did so in treatment. They came down to see him during family day, and from what I heard, there'd been a lot of tears. There'd been a lot of blame and people wondering if they could have prevented her influence. They couldn't possibly, of course, but hurting for him, they wanted to do so. Colton, deep in his healing, was able to explain to them it was no one's fault. Things happened, and it's what we did after that mattered the most. He'd told them about the reason behind his overdose then.

But that was only after he told me.

I didn't come down for that family visit because I came before that at Colton's request. He'd wanted to talk to me, and his counselors agreed he should. He wanted to explain to me what happened that night, just the two of us, as that had been how it all began.

"I don't believe I wanted to die that night, Cami," he said to me, completely vulnerable. He had unshed tears in his eyes, but I had already shed mine.

I cupped his face, waiting for him, and I was there when those tears finally fell. He'd looked up at me, gripping my hand with a flush in his cheeks.

"But if it happened," he explained, his eyes red. He squeezed my wrist tight. "I would have given in to it."

I had anticipated this, so much about that night still weighed on my heart. He'd had so much pain, and he didn't even have to tell me. I saw it. I *lived it* in that moment.

I held him close after that, both of us in a wash of so many emotions. It was the beginning of what was next for us.

Especially after what he said next.

"I love you, Camille," he said, before brushing his lips softly over mine. He held me closer. "And I'm finally brave enough to tell you."

Twenty-Three

CAMI

"Colton, where are your damn paper plates?"

Colton's quickening hips didn't stop at the sound of his pop's voice, and I had to keep my laughter silent. Buried deep inside me, the basketball player only braced my hips more, fucking me from inside his closet. His whole family was in the house somewhere, and we had to be stealthy about this.

I sighed as he pinched my lips between his, the man's scent rich and smoky from his aftershave. He'd shaved his head again after leaving treatment, but I didn't think for the same reasons this time.

I ran my hand over his buzz cut, his powerful hips slapping my inner thighs. His hips pumped, sweat beading his brow, and all too soon, he filled that condom between my legs.

I moaned as my orgasm hit, my hand slapping his closet door. With his whole family in the house for what felt like days, we'd had to sneak away for this moment.

But it was worth it.

Colton held my butt cheeks as we rode it out, not letting me go. His dad called again from somewhere downstairs, but the pair of us stayed silent, exhausted.

"Colton, honey. If you don't come out of that room and help your poppa find those plates so he can eat, I'm going to come up there!"

At his grandma Rose's voice, Colton laughed, pressing his mouth to mine to silence my own. She *couldn't* come up here, and that much was a given.

Together, we dropped away from his closet wall, and after putting himself away, Colton gathered my scattered clothes. I was naked from the waist down and had actually tried to resist this man's coercion for a quickie.

He was so just so very sexy.

Completely smoldering, Colton wore his jeans low on his hips. *He* was naked from the waist up, and my greedy eyes couldn't help but feast on his toned body and rippling abs. After he gave me my clothes, he found his, sliding on his t-shirt.

"Eh, uh, don't do that, Gram. I'm coming," he shouted behind himself, laughing, actually *laughing*, and it was so good to hear. He didn't laugh when he first came back, and it took a while for things to finally get back into a rhythm. I was happy things were turning around, and today definitely marked that.

His family was here with us for most of the week because they were packing him up. He was moving out, and I was going with him.

The pair of us honestly didn't know how Miami would react to him essentially getting sick after signing contracts. He was so fragile, but not only did they say they still wanted him, but they'd wait for him. The team reps said they'd wait as long as they needed to, and thankfully, that hadn't been long. Tonight was Colton's going-away party, the final step before our big move, and a large change for me as well. I'd be working for Roxie, Colton's sister-in-law, as soon as we got settled in.

I really did get it all in the end.

"Gram, just a sec," he tossed, opening the closet door. He waved me back, and I stood, grinning behind my hand.

"Colton—" she started again, but then Colton slid out of the closet, closing me in behind him.

"Gram, you didn't have to come all the way up here," I heard him say, and listening behind the door, I couldn't keep that smile off my face.

"What are you doing up here, honey? Where's Camille?"

"Oh, uh, she's around," he grunted. He definitely hadn't covered well, and my face burned.

"I thought y'all were packing," Colton's grandma continued. "You said you were going to pack up this room and there's barely any boxes filled."

I cringed, but still fought my laughter. We'd *started* to pack and then...

"Still working on it, Gram," Colton said, so obviously anxious with his heavy breath. "And tell Pop to ask Irene where the paper plates are. She packed most of the kitchen up last week."

Irene, though she wasn't coming with us, was with Colton until the end. She'd cried more in this last week than she had even after finding out Colton had been having mental health trouble, which had been a lot. Upon living with them both, I knew she saw Colton as another one of her children. She loved him, and I knew he'd miss her. I would too.

Pressing my ear to the door more, I strained to hear the tail end of the conversation, but it seemed Colton calmed his gram down enough for her to leave. I came out of the room after that, and the minute he saw me, he rushed over, grabbing me.

"Colton!"

He spun me around, dropping me on the bed that had already been ripped of its bedding. He somehow landed on top of me, and when he did, he pressed a big old kiss to my cheek.

"Have I told you how much I love you?" he asked me, less joking around when he moved to my lips. He actually couldn't *stop* telling me he loved me, not since we got back. He really wasn't afraid of it anymore, opening his heart and letting someone in. I'd learned that his lack of commitment came from the absence of his mom in his life, something he'd shared with me once he arrived home. I hadn't been surprised, and I think in the back of my mind, I maybe might have guessed that. He never kept women around, at least not long, and the ones he did, he couldn't seem to choose between, like he was scared to.

"Not as much as I love you," I said, breathing him in and tasting his tongue. He made me hot all over again, and we might have just gotten down one more time if not for his dad calling again. It seemed he couldn't find the cups this time, and judging by the smell of barbecue coming from downstairs, the man was *ready* to eat. He'd been cooking most of the day for Colton's going-away party. Colton had all his friends coming over later today. Jesse would attend, of course, and even Tommy would be there too, which made me happy. He wasn't coming to Miami, but only because a referral I gave him to one of the top PR firms in LA wanted him to work personally for them. It seemed I had some pull in this city after working for Colton. I'd made a mark, did a good job, and people were listening because of it.

Things really were going perfectly, and this man hovering above me was only the cherry on top.

"Be down in two seconds, Pop. Two seconds," Colton said, smiling a little before getting back to where we were. His hand moving up my thigh, Colton kissed me into a short oblivion.

"Give your girlfriend time to breathe, boy, and get your rear down here!"

My eyes wide at what his pop *clearly* knew was going on in

here, Colton and I both laughed. He let me up then, tugging me with him. I got to my feet and started to go so we didn't have to answer to his large father but stopped when Colton didn't immediately move. He was reading his phone and I walked over.

Hey, I'll never stop trying. I just wanted you to know that. I love you, Colt. I really do and I'm sorry, it said and I did read it over his shoulder. I saw no name with the number, but I knew who it was.

Colton did too obviously.

He deleted the text message immediately, then grabbed me in a nice firm hold. I knew he was beyond the crap that went down with his mom, but still, I knew it wasn't easy for him to see her reaching out. She had a couple times, never approached him, of course, but she had called, texted. She apparently wasn't giving up.

"You know, you don't need to respond to her," I said to him. I had explained what she said at the coffeehouse, what happened and why she hadn't been there for him. She did *seem* like she was ready to step up and be a good person, but the only one who could be the judge of that was this man.

He kissed the back of my hand, using it to pull my arm around his neck. He held me by my hips for a short millennium.

"Today isn't about that," he said, but his smile didn't quite reach his eyes. Bending down, he kissed me again, holding me close. Taking me by the hand, he led me outside his bedroom. I supposed, when it came to his mom, he was again moving past it.

∽

Colton

The amount of people who showed up for my send-off to Miami should have astounded me, but it didn't. I had so much support here, so many friends that turned into family. Having my own here amongst them only cemented all the good times I had in this city, my new family and my old coming together. I'd like to say I was nervous about leaving it all behind, uncomfortable, but I wasn't. I'd learned that change isn't a bad thing, that people could be there for you and be trusted. I was happy I got to learn those lessons all while living here, and I personally stopped and had full conversations with everyone in the room. I saw all my old teammates and even some new ones. I'd been down to Miami a couple times since I got back from treatment, and already, I was making more family down there. They came for this bash, hanging out with my brother Griff most of the time, but mingling too. My agent, Joe, even stopped by, and though he was staying here, he was representing me still. We'd be seeing each other monthly and even weekly in the beginning.

"I made this for you, and you better be eating while you're down there," said Irene, red in her eyes as she handed me a damn quilt. The thing looked handmade, and I was completely in awe.

"You didn't have to do this," I told her. I would miss her, truly a friend to me.

She cupped my cheek. "Take care of yourself," she said, and I brought her into the biggest hug. She'd cheered for me so hard in the end. I gave her a peck on the cheek before I had to leave her too and greet more people. My family was the life of the party, but ironically enough, not because of my all-star brother Griffin.

Brody literally had a circle around him, the rest of my family members with him, along with a bunch of my friends. My brother pointed at me when he saw me from across the room, and curious, I started to go over there, but my arm was grabbed.

"I wouldn't," Jesse said, cringing when he pulled me back. He clearly just arrived, as I hadn't seen him, and the motherfucker had the nerve to grab a beer before even saying hi to me first. That's classic Jesse, and I couldn't help but smile. He did too, jostling me with the bottle before pointing it in the direction of my family. "Your bro's telling embarrassing stories about you."

With that, a round of laughter shot out of that room, Brody the ringleader when he tossed an arm around his wife, Alexa. They'd left the twins at home and currently sat on my couch, Brody making a weird jiggle dance on it. This, of course, made *everyone* laugh, and though I didn't know the context, I now knew it had something to do with me. He had everyone in hysterics, Hayden and Karen especially. They were sans kids too, as were Roxie and Griffin, all choosing sitters. The group all sat around hamming it up, and Brody even had my pop laughing. My pop too had a beer from his easy chair, listening to the man's story. My stepmom, Ann, Gram, Aunt Robin, and some of the older members of my family were in a circle chatting, but they stopped long enough to have a laugh at my brother and his stories.

"Motherfucker," I said, but broke down in laughter as well in the end. I couldn't help it. I couldn't seem to keep the smile off my face these days. Things were just so good.

Obviously, realizing he hadn't said hi, my pal Jesse brought me into a hug. I'd be missing him too, possibly the most. We'd been through thick and thin together on our team, and though we'd play against each other on the court soon, it'd suck to be a plane ride away.

I actually hadn't seen much of him as of late. He'd been busy doing his own stuff, and of course, I had my own. Between dealing with my own mess and packing to leave, I guess we'd both been absent. He wanted to give me my time to deal with everything, and I appreciated it. He was here now, though, and I pounded his fist, leaving all *that* with my brother and his stories to talk with my friend a bit. We took our talk to the kitchen, and I chatted with him for a little while before I got distracted.

She just had that effect on me.

My girl... was a goddess, a true ride-or-die, and the fact I couldn't keep my eyes off her only added to her perfect package. Camille wore my favorite dress on her, a white one that made her breasts and thighs look fucking perfect. Her hair done up, she had all her brown curls in a lovely waterfall effect on the top of her head. She noticed me staring, in full conversation with her former assistant, Tommy. She was probably saying goodbye to him like I had been to the rest of the room.

She waved at me over her glass, and I waved back, a sudden nervousness in my gut I probably could explain, but it'd be there anyway despite what I had planned for tonight. She did that to me, made me nervousness in the best possible way.

"I still can't believe you're dating Cami," Jesse said, waving at her too. He knew we were and finally knew everything now. I'd been keeping all my drama from him too, and of course, he'd been more than accepting. In the back of my mind, though, I did feel some of his distance might have been because all this went down and he didn't know about it. He was my friend. He was *close*, and he still didn't see everything. I'd just been so good at hiding it.

I might have been mistaken, though, because none of that could be seen on this night. Jesse was more than casual, taking a drink, and all that was hopefully, thankfully in the past with us.

He took another sip of his beer, swallowing it down a little hard this time. "And you guys are still moving in together?"

"Yeah," I said, finally allowing my gaze to part from my

wonderful woman and return to my friend. "It all worked out, her getting that job with my sister-in-law and everything."

I was so proud of her. She was so damn special and she was with me. Hell, if I hadn't given her enough reasons to run away, but she didn't. She stayed.

"You think it'll all turn out?" Jesse asked me, my attention moving over to him. He frowned for some reason. "I guess I just mean Cami's cool people, and you've been indecisive in the past."

I might get offended if anyone else said that, but Jesse had seen a lot being friends with me. He had no reason to worry about Cami, though.

I was actually about to prove that to him.

Those nerves popped up again, and I asked Jesse for his drink. He gave it to me, looking curious, and I took it down hard.

"It will," I told him. "I just hope she says yes."

"Yes?"

I nodded, then handed him back his drink and headed in for the question of my life. I walked right over to Cami, taking her hand, and her eyes widened when I waved to get everyone's attention.

"Hey, Pop! Gram, Aunt Robin, everyone. If you can come in here, I have an announcement to make!" I called into the other room. "You too, Brody. I heard you were talking about me, you asshole!"

He had the nerve to look offended when he got up, leading the party from the living room. I got a look from both him *and* my gram after what I said, and I cringed at the connection.

"Sorry, Gram!" I said to her, dropping an arm around Cami. Camille laughed at me while most of the house made it into the kitchen. Filled to the brim, everyone who could fit in it did, and my brothers stood back so their wives could see.

Everyone really was here, my whole immediate family outside of the kiddos. It just made this moment that much more special, and I brought Camille closer.

She put an arm around my waist, happy to be a part of whatever this moment was. She really would be here for me through it all. She had been.

I faced the room. "I guess I just wanted to thank everyone for coming out, but not just that. You've all been here and not just through the good stuff. I wanted you all to know that I appreciate you, and you've made things not only easier but worthwhile."

A few raised their glasses to me, my brothers and Jesse lifting their beers. There were smiles all around me, but none wider than on the woman under my arm.

Camille had these big brown eyes I really could see now that I was this close, and just like that night on my couch, she lost me in her. She lost me in her essence, her goodness and her big heart. It was big *for* me and never closed me out, no matter how many times it should have.

"I shouldn't have you," I said to her, this room frickin' full, but I could only see her. I squeezed her shoulder. "But since I do, since *you've* allowed me..."

I had to drop to one knee before she realized what was going on, and the entire room, the women mostly, gasped, chants of glee sprinkling around us. The room went silent after that, and it was only Cami and me.

I pulled the diamond ring I bought for her out, the one *only* for her. I never thought I'd marry anyone, but then came her.

"Oh, God. No, you're not," she gasped, her hands pressing to her mouth. They fell from her lips. "Colton Chandler, you are not—"

"I am," I said, opening the box. The emerald cut sparkled,

shined as bright as her eyes, filling with emotions. "If you'll let me, that is. Cami, will you marry me?"

She actually left me hanging for a second, looking around the room. She stopped on my family. "Is it okay?" she asked *them*, and something about that warmed my heart. She knew how much they meant to me, and she'd spent a lot of time with them during my recovery. We'd been a true family, and she was a part of it. She smiled with tear-filled eyes at them all. "Because I really want to be a part of your family."

My gram's hands moved to her chest, and my aunt Robin was actually crying. In fact, all the women in my family were in hysterics.

I let the feeling fall away that one was absent, one closer to home, and waited too. This moment was the most important, not my past. No, my mother wasn't here, but that was okay. I didn't need her. Just Cami and all the other special people in my life.

One of them smiled, my gram. "We'd be happy to have you, honey. So happy."

My pop put an arm around her, and Cami, well, there was no more resistance. She bent down and kissed me, the yes on her lips, and I slipped the ring on her finger as the room erupted in applause.

Everyone was here for this big moment, all the people I cared about. I danced Cami around after she said yes. When her feet touched the floor, we were together.

"I can't believe you did this. How did you do this? Ah!" she shouted at me, admiring the ring before she kissed me. "I love you."

"I love you, too," I said, then a small tidal wave of my family swarmed us. They crowded around us, the women wanting to see the ring and the men congratulating me.

"She's a good one," my pop said, then faced the ladies. "It seems they think so too."

I was happy for that, literally all my female family members dancing around her. I got hugs from my brothers, a fist pound from a few friends, but one of them I noticed was absent. I didn't see Jesse immediately after the proposal, and since he'd been acting weird, his question about Cami and all that, I decided to go find him. I headed over to Cami first.

"I'll be right back," I told her, kissing her on the cheek. "I lost Jess in the shuffle. Need to go find him."

"Is everything okay?" she asked, and as I hoped so, I put on a smile for her. She was quickly surrounded by people after I left, folks wanting to see the ring, and I wasn't terribly worried about her as I circled my packed-up house. There were a lot of places he could go, but I figured if he was anywhere, it'd be in the pool house. The extra booze was out there, and it wouldn't be uncommon for me to find him there during a party when the drinks got low.

That's probably all this is.

Putting my hood up, I headed out there. It was misting outside, the evening settling in, and my property's back lighting triggered on as I walked. The light to the pool house was illuminated on the outside, and I had hope he was in there.

"Jess?" I stated, pulling my hood down with when I walked inside. As it was dark, I flicked on a light. I saw him staring out the windows toward the back at the Hills. I picked up my feet. "Jess, what's going on?"

He didn't talk to me. He didn't... move, and it wasn't until I got over to him that I understood why. He had something in his hands, something I recognized.

The nine-millimeter came from my house, usually in my study. I bought it at a gun show a while back and figured it didn't hurt to have one in the house. I grew up around guns, being from Texas, but it usually never made it out the lockbox.

Jesse had it for some reason, Jesse *my friend* who wouldn't look at me at the present.

"Jess?" I said, slow because I really didn't understand what was going on. I just knew what my body was telling me, my instincts. My heart was racing and... *that* I noticed.

His eyes closed slow. "Why did you come out here, Colton?"

I swallowed, daring to get closer. He only had the gun in his hand, palming it with the other. I lifted my hand but was casual about it. "You found my gun?"

His lips twitched a little, a humorless smile. "You know I know where it is."

I did, so I nodded. I'd shown it to him. He came from the rural South, so he wasn't unfamiliar with guns either. It'd been a quick show and not a big deal.

Even more casual, I leaned against the window, folding my arms so he could see me. We stood by each other, and I didn't do anything rash.

"Hey, um, Jess, we should probably go back in, don't you think? Did you see the proposal? I'm, um, engaged, man." And for some reason, these felt like the wrong words to say. My friend actually... cringed when I said that, cringed like I hurt him or burned him. I moved, and he braced that gun, making me halt.

"Yeah, I saw," he said, tapping the pistol to the air. "You just don't."

Not understanding, I shook my head, and with the gun in hand, he drew his hands down his messy hair. It was all weathered from the rain, and he looked disheveled, a mess, and it didn't help my buddy was armed.

He smiled a little but looked sad about it. "I actually thought it was all like me, your situation, you..." He laughed a little, finally facing me. "You fuck all these women, mess around like I do... A front."

"A front—"

"I'm in love with you, Colton."

I froze in my steps, shock rattling me. There's no way he said what he just had. He... loved me? How so...

But as I watched him, the fear suddenly rampant in his eyes, I think I knew in what way. I knew the *reality* of it. Even if I didn't get it at first, see it.

"You..." I paused, still trying to make sense of the words. "You *love* me—"

"Just forget I said it. Just... Oh, God." The fear transformed, the man petrified in all the ways one could be. I think *he* just figured out what he said to me.

And what that meant for both of us.

He said something I never realized about himself and something he clearly had hopes for. He said he thought I was like him.

When I so obviously wasn't.

I'd seen no signs, *all of this* coming out of left field, and I didn't know what to do or say, and he saw that. He *saw* my hesitance, my drawback, and he lifted that gun...

But he didn't lift it at me.

He raised it to his head, his intent crystal clear, and I should have talked him down. I shouldn't have moved, but I did. I didn't want him to take the out. I wanted him to fight. I wanted him to *be*.

I needed him to for himself.

My hands up, I eased toward him. I *moved* toward him. "Jesse, no..."

"Stay back, Colton. Just..." His eyes red, they brimmed with emotion, actual tears filling them. "I can't. I... Just go back to your party, Colt."

"I won't. I'm here with you, man. In this moment here and now. I'm not leaving."

His jaw moved, his finger on the trigger. "Why?"

I lowered my hands. "Because you need me to be," I said, making him hear it. "And I need you in my life, too."

The world needed us both. I used to be so alone in my lies. I boxed myself in and couldn't see what was truly around me, a world that needed me and one I wanted to be a part of.

It took me a while to understand that, lots of therapy, but once I'd seen it, I wasn't letting go and I wasn't going to let him go either.

My words rattled him, made his hands shake. He lowered the gun, those tears actually falling down his cheeks. I'd never once seen this man cry. Neither of us did, but it seemed things were starting to change. I also shared vulnerability and emotions not that long ago.

And thank God for that.

His gun down, I approached him, and after he gave it to me, I placed it down. I gave him a hug after that, something my pop gave me when I'd been in my own depths. I hadn't known I needed it until then, and that moment had been the beginning of the next chapter of my life, the real start of my recovery.

"I'm so sorry, Colt," Jesse said, his voice laced with emotion in my ear. He squeezed me hard. "I'm so sorry I..."

"I need you, buddy," I said, gripping his shoulder. "I need you in my life, but it won't be enough. You gotta want that for yourself."

His nod was firm, and we stayed in that moment.

I'd stay as long as he needed me to.

Twenty-Four

COLTON

I HAD a lot of miles ahead of me, and I was happy to say I got to do a lot of them with one of my best friends. My trip with Jesse to San Francisco was a special one and something I think he needed too. He talked to me during those miles, told me everything. His feelings hadn't always been there, and he did fight them for as long as he could. No one knew he was gay. No one in the industry or even back home where he was from, Mississippi. He locked away that part of himself for a long time, and though he had a strong indication his feelings weren't reciprocated by me, our friendship allowed him to think more. He couldn't help it. He wanted so badly for it that he made it so in his head. I told him that was okay, that *he* was okay. We were still friends and always would be. I dropped him off at his own treatment after that, a place he'd found by himself. He wanted help to not be scared of who he was anymore. He wanted to be okay, and hopefully, one day he would be. He shouldn't be locked away anymore.

The world deserved to know him.

I was happy for that time I got with him, that send-off as I got to move on toward my next chapter. My girl—well, I guess fiancée—now knew I'd be gone for a few hours longer after my trip with Jesse. I had another stop to make while in town, and I made it slow.

I pulled up to the section of housing in one of San Francisco's projects, where my mom lived. Maggie had actually moved to California to be closer to me, something she admitted in the texts since the incident at the coffeehouse. She wanted to be near but not too close.

She wanted this moment today.

Coming to her was for me, though. *Finally*, I was doing something for myself and not for her. That's how things ended up being with her, my desire to help and be there for her. I came with a curiosity when I should have stuck around for what I needed. I was doing that today.

She was outside when I pulled up, my rental car modest so as to not gain attention. After the coffeehouse, I'd been in the tabloids for weeks. They eventually let go, and a lot of that had to do with my PR people, Cami. Knowing exactly what to do, they fed the media their own stories, and eventually, it all died away. However, it all turned out I didn't care, as I'd been busy with other things surrounding my mental health, but I was happy it worked out. I'd be getting that fresh start I wanted once I got to Miami.

I hoped today I'd get another one.

Maggie did look good when I came over, just like she had in the coffeehouse. Toward the end of our meet-ups, she'd looked very much like she slid back into her old habits, but now... I think she was clean and maybe in more ways than one. She had a clarity in her eyes, like she was ready for the world to see her.

She smiled at me, so lovely that I couldn't believe she'd ever struggled. I hated for a while that my brothers and I looked the most like her, but I didn't now.

"Hi," she said.

"Hi," I said, my hands in my pockets.

Nervous, she gazed around a bit before pointing behind herself. "You wanna go inside or..."

"Uh, no, that's okay. This is a quick stop."

I could tell she didn't know what to do with that, her face trying to mask a wave of emotions with her smile. I did walk over to her door, though, but only for more privacy. There weren't a lot of people outside but enough.

"How have you been?" she asked, leaning against her door. "I saw in the press you're about to start soon, Miami to play with Griff?"

I wasn't surprised she watched me, watched us. She probably knew a lot about all of us, even my other brothers who weren't in the papers.

I acknowledged what she said with a nod, but not much else, kicking the ground.

"Colton, I'm so sorry about what happened. I told your friend—"

"I know," I told her. I knew everything. Cami had told me everything that went down between her and Maggie, but I wasn't here for that. "I do, but I need to tell you something."

"Anything," she said, stepping forward. So much hope in her eyes. She really did want this, a relationship with me. Maybe even more than I had. I was happy that was the case and felt more secure about being here because of it. I didn't need her.

But I wanted her in my life.

"I don't need you to be a part of my life," I said, but didn't mean it in a cruel way. It was just facts. I looked at her, swallowing hard. "But I want you there. I want to know you, to get to know you."

"I want that too." She smiled. "That's all I ever wanted. Things just got messed up. I messed things up."

She had, but I helped her. She hadn't been alone in all this, the enabling.

"The family, my brothers and everybody, knows you're around. I told them all before coming here," I said. "They know, and this, us talking, isn't going to include them. They aren't a part of this. It's just you and me."

"That's okay. I think that's best anyway, at first."

"It'll be slow," I said, being honest. "You and I will be slow, and I just... I need time to trust you."

It might take a hella long time, but I was willing to put in the work if she was. I didn't care about her story before or even ours when we initially reunited. Our beginnings were so far back in my mind, but not because she deserved forgiveness or anything else. It was because being weighed down by history served no one. She might not have deserved my forgiveness but she was getting it anyway because that's what I wanted. That's what was best for me, for my healing.

I was finally healing.

She told me that was okay, that I could take all the time I needed. She was willing to do whatever she had to, and I was happy.

"Did everything work out with your friend?" she asked after it was all said and done, and the smile, it was full on her face this time. We were on the cusp of our new beginning, the right one. She tilted her head. "The one that came to see me? You said you loved her."

I did love Camille, my everything. I literally wouldn't be here if it wasn't for her two times over.

My smile was genuine too. "I asked her to marry me."

Maggie's eyes lit up, her nod firm. "And what did she say?"

"Maybe you should ask her," I told her, nodding. "Because she wants to start over with you too."

Twenty-Five

CAMI

Not long later...

"I NOW PRONOUNCE you man and wife... again!"

Colton's brother Brody was a big kid. At the announcement signaling the end of the vow renewal, he picked up his wife, Alexa, exclaiming a bright and vibrant, "Hell yeah!" before smacking her right on the lips in front of everyone. This got a few gasps from the crowd, one of which was the boys' grandmother.

Colton's grandma Rose gasped, her hand to her chest, and I noticed Colton's aunt Robin nudge her a little, laughing and telling her mama to loosen up.

"Brody!" Alexa chided in response to her husband, apparently not a fan of the cursing in front of their children. The twin girls Gabby and Riley stood beside their parents, and the eldest Chandler brother, Hayden, was the officiant. Apparently, he got ordained just for the day, wanting to be a part of this moment, as none of the family had the first time around.

From what I learned, Brody and Alexa had opted for a speed wedding right before their children were born. They wanted it done right this time, and what could be more right than the place where their family spent so much of their lives?

The Chandler ranch was lively today, the second wedding ever to be held there. Colton's brother Griffin and Roxie had married here as well, so I guess the vow renewal had been fitting.

Brody chuckled upon displeasing his wife, giving Alexa another smack on the lips before reaching down and kissing his girls. They each got a peck on the cheek before he picked them up, the mountainous hills of Texas behind them all. Colton's pop had done the wedding arch, beautiful and picturesque when combined with the lovely landscape behind. They even had a pink flower at the top of the arch, their grandma Rose's favorite flowers.

There were hints of her everywhere here today, on the pews and in the distance at the adorned barn where the reception would be held tonight. Brody had wanted to honor her, the matriarch of the family. Even the men wore Grandma Rose's flowers as boutonnieres, strong men behind Brody. They went in descending order as far as ages, my man on the end there and looking just as sexy and mouthwatering as he ever had. Colton had allowed his curls to grow back recently, wild and just as untamed as he was. They blew in the wind, making him even more handsome than normal in his pressed suit. He had a Stetson hat in his hands, as did all the men during the ceremony.

Catching my eye, Colton winked at me, and I shook my head at him. My attention shifted when Hayden presented Brody and Alexa and I stood, clapping with everyone else at the bride and groom. The happy couple each took one of their kids, taking them hand in hand before heading down the aisle. Returning their hats to their heads, Griffin and Colton brought up the rear. Upon coming to Roxie, Griffin immediately grabbed his wife's hand, their little one, Jackson, coming with them, and Colton grabbed my hand. This was all a part of the ceremony, all the Chandler kids a part of this moment.

Colton threw an arm over my shoulder, being his silly self, and how I loved him for it. There were times not so long ago where he lost that.

I was happy to say they were far behind us.

He enjoyed today, his whole family did, as this was one of the many beautiful reasons they came together. Though Colton and I were still engaged, I'd been fortunate enough to already become a part of this family and see *family* in its truest form around me. I couldn't wait to combine his and mine together. My parents were separated, but they'd love to be a part of this too. Who wouldn't? Colton's family loved each other and made me feel just as much a part of that home despite the fact Colton and I hadn't had our union yet. This was next to come, though. We planned for next spring.

Bringing up the rear of the Chandler parade was Colton's pop and stepmom, Ann. They had Hayden's girls in chairs beside them before they all rose and joined us. The girls threw flowers, and we were all on our way, friends and family all around us. I'd never seen such community as I had while being amongst this brood.

So much love was in the air, and it took us into the evening, my fiancé on my arm as we moved into dance upon dance. The barn was hopping, and everyone was on their feet the entire time. No song played without the dance floor full. Toward the end when things got quiet and the night started to fall, I fell into my most happy place.

Colton placed a hand on the small of my back, telling me how much he loved me, while his brothers slow-danced with their spouses around us. Some even had their children in the dance, warming my heart.

I envisioned this would be us soon, all these wonderful people setting the groundwork for us. From what I understood, Colton and I had a lot to live up to, like the great loves on this dance floor tonight. I spent much of the evening just watching Colton's pop and Ann, who were truly inspiring. Very few moments went by when he didn't have eyes on her.

"Are we getting married here too?" I asked, lifting my head from Colton's lapels. He'd never looked so handsome, free. His hair may have been windblown and he may have retired his hat and suit jacket around the third or fourth song, but he never looked so perfect.

He made me feel that way as well, on his arm and his hands on me in ways that made me feel like I was the only one he'd ever touch. Maybe in the end, the last one was the only one that mattered anyway.

"If you want to," he told me, chuckling a little before facing his family. They were sprinkled all around us, again that dance floor filled. He faced me. "But I warn you, if you let them take hold, it might not be our wedding anymore."

Laughing, I pressed my cheek to his chest. "That might not be so bad."

He squeezed my hand, his mouth warming the top of my head. "You might be right about that."

It might just be all a little bit perfect, our wedding becoming theirs. So much about today had been so wonderful I nearly missed when the air had changed. It wasn't until our dance stopped a little, slowed down, and the floor opened up.

I saw a woman across the room, one I knew my fiancé had been in contact with. He hadn't given up on his mom, and I hadn't either. We spoke to Maggie from time to time. It'd been a long process, but she was there, present in both his life and mine. As far as I knew, she hadn't been a part of the rest of the Chandlers' world, though, and I looked at Colton.

"I invited her," he said, pulling away from me a little. "And everyone knows I did. Everyone's okay with it."

I watched the world open up, each couple become aware of the new arrival. Maggie looked lovely in her pink dress, Grandma Rose's... *her mom's* favorite color.

Grandma Rose saw her, standing shakily from her chair with the assistance of Colton's aunt Robin. As far as I knew, there had been no contact between them during the many years passed.

Grandma stared at her, her head tilted. She may have been warned about today, but the fact didn't make her any less emotional at seeing her daughter.

Maggie walked over to her, wrestling her hands. The moment they finally met, I couldn't hear what was said as Colton and I were so far away...

But I saw the hug.

We *all* did. It'd been quickly engaged too, Grandma Rose the reason. The older woman hugged Maggie tight, and soon, Robin joined in too, Maggie's sister.

"Are you going to go over?" I asked Colton, and he shook his head.

"This is their time," he said, sliding back into the dance with me, and I noticed his brothers did the same. Of course they noticed their mom as well, took inventory, but in the end, they went for the same position as their younger brother. They got back together with their spouses, the dance continuing, and even though Colton's pop was aware of Maggie, his ex-wife, he too took up where he'd left off. He danced with his own wife, stayed with *her*. There would no doubt be talking later, for things *later* to happen. There was a lot of pain in this room because of Maggie, a lot of history, but in that moment, there was tranquility.

There were just sisters, a mom and her daughters. There were three people who hadn't seen each other in a long time, and the Chandler men and their wives were all letting them have that moment. They were putting others' needs first before their own, and I wasn't surprised. That was the family I would soon be entering into...

And I couldn't wait.

Epilogue

COLTON

One Year Later

THE CROWD BUZZED in the stadium, the energy flowing through my veins even from the locker room. My new team chanted as well, all of us huddled in a circle as a unit. We'd said our prayers, allowed those blessings to flow through the air, and now... it was time to do this.

We broke with a war cry, heading out to the arena.

The fans didn't let us down.

The room dimmed, the Miami stadium filled with spectators' light, cellphones in the stands like twinkling stars, and one by one, the announcer called us players in. My teammates and I got to drink in all that fan energy, our biggest supporters with us during each and every win. We hadn't lost a game since I got here last year, and though the arrogant son of a bitch beside me—my brother Griffin—could take a lot of credit for that, I'd give credit where credit was due. We were all fucking badasses.

I just happened to be related to the one who reigned supreme.

Griff had helped me so much with my transition here, given me a connection to blood while I played the game I loved. Having him, Roxie, and Jackson alongside my move here with Cami had just been the icing on the cake for an experience I never should have let become obstructed by my own demons. I used to get in my own way but no more.

Griffin slammed his hands down on my shoulders from behind, buzzing just as much as the crowd out there in the arena. He didn't say anything about his nerves prior to this moment, but he had to have them. Tonight was a big night, a huge one for him. Squeezing my shoulders, he remained patient while each and every one of our teammates were called to the court. The pair of us were last. They usually announced by alphabetical order before a game, but again, tonight was special. It was my brother's final game, his final night on the court. He had decided to retire early to fully immerse himself in Pop's business and, eventually, move back to Texas where it all began. I was nervous about that, being on my own after playing alongside him, but then, I realized I didn't need to be. He left me some awesome stuff here.

Now, I just had to take it.

"You nervous, Mini Me?" he asked, his nickname for me as kids. He used to use it all the time, and I'd never admit I missed that. I'd miss this guy a lot, my all-star brother.

I cocked my head. "You?" I asked, nudging him.

My name called, I charged out to center court, and the fans roared at my arrival, roared for me. I'd had a good run here so far, and a lot of that had to do with that blue backlight.

Cami made her cellphone light blue on purpose, making it so I'd always see her. She waved her signal at me, and I found her immediately courtside.

Shaking her light, I saw her smile and those lips I couldn't wait to kiss tonight. We were freshly newlyweds, our wedding fucking explosive a few months ago, and folks were still talking about it. We didn't end up getting married at my gram's ranch, but in Bali. We'd always been kind of different, but people showed. They cared about us and wanted to be there. We had to make it quick since Griff and I had games back in the States, but that had been okay too. Cami had been my support system through all of this, and I was hers. She was quickly climbing up the ladder at Roxie's firm, living out her own path.

The two of us were a team, and tonight, my other supporters clustered around her.

I knew by the signs.

My family's were always the biggest and illuminated as well. Today, *Go Griff* + *We love our boys!* shimmered right in my eyes. The entire crew was there, Pop and my stepmom, Ann, Gram and Aunt Robin, as well as my brothers and their wives, along with their kids. Roxie, of course, had Jackson tonight too, the boy on her shoulders to see his poppa's final game. I panned, and the final person I looked for I easily spotted. She'd come to many of our games, so many despite her living across the country.

Momma, our mom, never took anything from us. She hadn't since she arrived back into our lives. There'd been a lot of tears at Brody's vow renewal last year, a lot of pain, and though it'd taken a lot of time, we were all getting there. Maggie was making her way back to us, and though developing a solid relationship with her wouldn't occur overnight, all my brothers were willing, even our pop. She'd hurt him, yes, but that pain eased a little upon the arrival of my stepmom, Ann. He was so happy now, Ann his true soul mate. All of us Chandlers had literally moved to new heights, gotten over hurdles and found our happiness. The only link to us who hadn't was our mom... Momma.

We felt she deserved a second chance too.

She raised her sign higher when Griff came out, and there was a reason I got to be announced right before him. He was passing on the torch to me, and the stadium blew up for this moment, his final walk he made toward his younger bro.

He lifted his hand to me in center court, literally ready to hand things off. His legacy was now mine. I had a lot to live up to, but I was ready. I wanted that honor and to prove to him I was worthy of it.

I took his hand, and the crowd roared, my brother bringing me into a hug. We were about to play our final game together, and to make this whole evening even more perfect, it'd be against my old pal Jesse. He'd been traded to NYC, something he wanted after he finally got back on the court himself after treatment. He'd ended up meeting his boyfriend in his new city.

And goddamn was I happy for him.

Things had turned out so well for all of us, and I hoped my friend was prepared for tonight. He was about to go against not one, but two Chandler men, and I had to say...

He better be ready.

Click the link below to download book one of the Love in the City series!

Download on Amazon